'What are you doing?' Miller demanded in a furious whisper.

Valentino stared down at her, watching the pulse-point in her neck pick up speed. His body hummed with sexual need and he wondered what it was about her he found just so damned tempting.

'Why, Miller, I'm just doing what you asked. I'm going to make this farce of a relationship look more authentic.'

Before she could unload on him he took full advantage of her open mouth and planted his own firmly over the top of hers in a kiss.

All day he'd wondered if she'd taste as good as her summery scent promised and now he had his answer.

Better.

So much better.

From as far back as she can remember **Michelle Conder** has dreamed of being a writer. She penned the first chapter of a romance novel just out of high school, but it took much study, many (varied) jobs, one ultra-understanding husband and three very patient children before she finally sat down to turn that dream into reality.

Michelle lives in Australia, and when she isn't busy plotting loves to read, ride horses, travel and practise yoga.

Recent titles by the same author:

HIS LAST CHANCE AT REDEMPTION
GIRL BEHIND THE SCANDALOUS REPUTATION

Did you know these are also available as eBooks?
Visit www.millsandboon.co.uk

LIVING THE CHARADE

BY
MICHELLE CONDER

MILLS
BOON

First published in Great Britain 2013
by Mills & Boon, an imprint of Harlequin (UK) Limited.
Harlequin (UK) Limited, Eton House, 18-24 Paradise Road, Richmond, Surrey TW9 1SR

© Michelle Conder 2013

ISBN: 978 0 263 23416 9

Harlequin (UK) policy is to use papers that are natural, renewable and recyclable products and made from wood grown in sustainable forests. The logging and manufacturing process conform to the legal environmental regulations of the country of origin.

Printed and bound in Great Britain
by CPI Antony Rowe, Chippenham, Wiltshire

LIVING THE CHARADE

To my fabulous editor, Flo,
for encouraging me to try new things,
and to Paul, for his endless love.
You both make all the difference!

CHAPTER ONE

IF the world was a fair place the perfect solution to Miller Jacobs's unprecedented crisis would walk through the double-glazed doors of the hip Sydney watering hole she was in, wearing a nice suit and sporting an even nicer personality.

Unlike the self-important banker currently sitting at the small wooden table opposite her who probably should have stopped drinking at least two hours ago.

'So, sexy lady, what is this favour you need from me?'

Miller tried not to cringe at the man's inebriated state and turned to her close friend, Ruby Clarkson, with a smile that said, *How could you possibly think this loser would be in any way suitable as my fake boyfriend this coming weekend*?

Ruby arched a brow in apology and then did what only a truly beautiful woman could do—dazzled the banker with a megawatt smile and told him to take a hike. Not literally, of course. Chances were she'd have to work with him at some point in the future.

Miller breathed a sigh of relief as, without argument, he swaggered towards the packed, dimly lit bar and disappeared from view.

'Don't say it,' Ruby warned. 'On paper he seemed perfect.'

'On paper most men seem perfect,' Miller said glumly. 'It's only when you get to know them that the trouble starts.'

'That's morose. Even for you.'

Miller's eyebrows shot up. She had good reason to be feeling morose. She had just wasted an hour she didn't have, drinking white wine she wouldn't even cook with, and was no further towards solving her problem than she'd been yesterday. A problem that had started when she'd lied to her boss about having a boyfriend who would *love* to come away for a business weekend and keep a very important and very arrogant potential client in check.

TJ Lyons was overweight, overbearing and obnoxious, and had taken her 'not interested' signs as some sort of personal challenge. Apparently he had told Dexter, her boss, that he believed Miller's cool, professional image was hiding a hot-blooded woman just begging to be set free and he was determined to add her to his stable of 'fillies'.

Miller shuddered as she recalled overhearing him use that particular phrase.

The man was a chauvinistic bore and wore an Akubra hat as if he was Australia's answer to JR Ewing. But he had her rattled. And when TJ had challenged her to 'bring your hubbie' to his fiftieth birthday celebration, where she would also present her final business proposal, Miller had smiled sweetly and said that would be lovely.

Which meant she now needed a man by tomorrow afternoon. Perhaps she'd been a little hasty in giving Mr Inebriated the flick.

Ruby rested her chin in her hand. 'There's got to be someone else.'

'Why don't I just say he's sick?'

'Your boss is already suss on you. And even if he wasn't, if you give your *fake* boyfriend a *fake* illness, you still have to deal with your amorous client all weekend.'

Miller pulled a face. 'Don't mistake TJ's intentions as amorous. They're more licentious in nature.'

'Maybe so, but I'm sure Dexter's are amorous.'

Ruby was convinced Miller's boss was interested in her, but Miller didn't see it.

'Dexter's married.'

'Separated. And you know he's keen on you. That's one of the reasons you lied about having a boyfriend.'

Miller let her head fall back on her neck and made a tortured sound through her teeth.

'I was coming off the back of a week of sixteen-hour days and I was exhausted. I might have had an emotional reaction to the whole thing.'

'Emotional? You? Heaven forbid.' Ruby shivered dramatically.

It was a standing joke between them that Ruby wore her heart on her sleeve and Miller kept hers stashed in one of the many shoeboxes in her closet.

'I was after sympathy, not sarcasm,' Miller grumped.

'But Dexter did offer to go as your "protector", did he not?' Ruby probed.

Miller sighed. 'A little weird, I grant you, but we knew each other at uni. I think he was just being nice, given TJ's drunken pronouncements to him the week before.'

Ruby did her famous eye roll. 'Regardless, you faked having a boyfriend and now you have to produce one.'

'I'll give him pneumonia.'

'Miller, TJ Lyons is a business powerhouse with a shocking reputation and Dexter is an alpha male wannabe. And you've worked too hard to let either one of them decide your future. If you go away this weekend and TJ makes a move on you his wife will have a fit and you'll be reading the unemployment pages for the next twelve months. I've seen it happen before. Men of TJ Lyons's ilk are never pinned for sexual harassment the way they should be.'

Ruby took a breath and Miller thanked God that she needed air. She was one of the best discrimination lawyers in the country and when she ranted Miller took note. She had a point.

Miller had put in six hard years at the Oracle Consulting Group, which had become like a second home to her. Or maybe it *was* her home, given how much time she spent there! If she won TJ's multi-million-dollar account she'd be sure to be made partner in the next sweep—the realisation of a long-held dream and one her mother had encouraged for a long time.

'TJ hasn't actually harassed me, Rubes,' she reminded her friend.

'At your last meeting he said he'd hire Oracle in a flash if you "played nice".'

Miller blew out a breath. 'Okay, okay. I have a plan.'

Ruby raised her eyebrows. 'Let's hear it.'

'I'll hire an escort. Look at this.' The idea had come to her while Ruby had been ranting and she turned her smartphone so Ruby could see the screen. 'Madame Chloe. She says she offers discreet, professional, *sensitive* gentlemen to meet the needs of the modern-day heterosexual woman.'

'Let me see that.' Ruby took the phone. 'Oh, my God. That guy would seriously have sex with you.'

Miller looked over Ruby's shoulder at the incredibly buffed male on the screen.

'And they cater to fantasies!' Ruby continued.

'I don't *want* him to have sex with me,' Miller yelped, slightly exasperated. The last thing she needed was sex, or her hormones, to derail her from her goal at the eleventh hour. Her mother had let that happen and look where it had got her—broke and unhappy.

'You can have a policeman, a pilot, an accountant—*urgh*, seen enough of them. Oh, and this one.' Ruby giggled and lowered her voice. 'Rough but clean tradesman. Or, wait—a sports jock.'

Miller shuddered. What intelligent woman would ever fantasise over a sports jock?

'Ruby!' Miller laughed as she took the phone back. 'Be serious. This is my future we're talking about. I need a decent guy who is polite and can follow my lead. Someone who blends in.'

'Hmmm…' Ruby grinned at one of the profile photos. 'He looks like he would blend in at an all-night gay bar.'

Miller scowled. 'Not helping.' She clicked on a few more. 'They all look the same,' she said despairingly.

'Tanned, buff and hot-to-trot,' Ruby agreed. 'Where *do* they get these guys?'

Miller shook her head at Ruby's obvious enjoyment. Then she saw the price tag associated with one of the men. 'Good God, I hope that's for a month.'

'Forget the escort,' Ruby instructed. 'Most of these guys probably can't string a sentence together beyond "Is that it?" and "How hard do you want it?"' Not exactly convincing boyfriend material for an up-and-coming partner in the fastest growing management consultancy firm in Australia.'

'Then I'm cooked.'

Ruby's eyes scanned the meagre post-work crowd, and Miller thought about the sales report she still had to get through before bed that night; she was still unable to completely fathom the predicament she was in.

'Bird flu?' she suggested, smoothing her eyebrows into place as she racked her brain for a solution.

'No one will believe he has bird flu.'

'I meant me.' She sighed.

'Wait. What about him?'

'Who?' Miller glanced at her phone and saw only a blank screen.

'Cute guy at the bar. Three o'clock.'

Miller rolled her eyes. 'Five years of university, six years in a professional career and we're still using hushed military terms when stalking guys.'

Ruby laughed. 'It's been ages since we stalked a guy.'

'And, please God, let it be ages again,' Miller pleaded, glancing ever so casually in the direction Ruby indicated.

She got an impression of a tall man leaning against the edge of the curved wooden bar, one foot raised on the polished foot pole, his knee protruding from the hole in his torn jeans. Her eyes travelled upwards over long, lean legs and an even leaner waist to a broad chest covered by a worn T-shirt with a provocative slogan plastered on the front in red block letters. Her lips curled in distaste at its message and she moved on to wide shoulders, a jaw that looked as if it could have used a shave three days ago, a strong blade of a nose, mussed over long chocolate-brown hair and—oh, Lord—deep-set light-coloured eyes that were staring right back at her.

His gaze was sleepy, almost indolent, and Miller's heart took off. Her breath stalled in her lungs and her face felt bitingly hot. Flustered by her physical reaction, she instantly dropped her eyes as if she was a small child who had just been caught stealing a cookie. Her senses felt muddled and off-centre—and she'd only been looking at the man for five seconds. Maybe ten.

Ignoring the fact that she felt as if he was still watching her, she turned to Ruby. 'He's got holes in his jeans and a T-shirt that says "My pace or yours?" How many glasses of this crap wine have you had?'

Ruby paused, glancing briefly back at the bar. 'Not him—although he does fill that T-shirt out like a god. I'm talking about the suit he's talking to.'

Miller turned her gaze to the suit she hadn't noticed. Similar-coloured hair, square, clean-shaven jaw, nice nose, *great* suit. Yes, thankfully he did look more her type.

'Oh, I think I know him!' Ruby exclaimed.

'You *know* Ripped Jeans?'

'No.' Ruby shook her head, openly smiling in the direction Miller dared not turn back to. 'The hotshot in the suit beside him. Sam someone. I'm pretty sure he's a lawyer out of our L.A. office. And he's just the type you need.'

Miller glanced back and noticed that tall, dark and dishevelled was no longer watching her, but still some inner instinct told her to run. *Fast.*

'No!' She dismissed the idea outright. 'I draw the line at picking up a stranger in a bar—even if you do think you know him. Let me just go to the bathroom and then we can share a taxi home. And stop looking at those guys. They'll think we want to be picked up.'

'We do!'

Miller scowled. 'Believe me, by the look of the one who

needs to become reacquainted with a razor all it would take is a look and he'd have you horizontal in seconds.'

Ruby eyed her curiously. 'That's exactly what makes him so delicious.'

'Not to me.' Miller headed for the bathroom, feeling slightly better now that she had decided to call it a night. Her problem still hovered over her like a dark cloud, but she was too tired to give it any more brainpower tonight.

'Would you stop looking at those women? We are not here to pick up,' Tino Ventura growled at his brother.

'Seems to me it might solve your problem about what to do with yourself this weekend.'

Tino snorted. 'The day I need my baby brother to sort entertainment for me is the day you can put me in a body bag.'

Sam didn't laugh, and Tino silently berated his choice of words.

'So how's the car shaping up?' Sam asked.

Tino grunted. 'The chassis still needs work and the balancing sucks.'

'Will it be ready by Sunday?'

The concern in his brother's voice set Tino's teeth on edge. He was so *over* everyone worrying about this next race as if it was to be his last—and okay, there were a couple of nasty coincidences that made for entertaining journalism, but they weren't *signs*, for God's sake.

'It'll be ready.'

'And the knee?'

Coming off the back of a long day studying engine data and time trials in his new car, Tino was too tired to humour his brother with shop-talk.

'This catch-up drink was going a lot better before you started peppering me with work questions.'

He could do without the reminder of how his stellar racing year had started to fall apart lately. All he needed was to win

this next race and he'd have the naysayers who politely suggested that he would never be as good as his father off his back.

Not that he dwelt on their opinion.

He didn't.

But he'd still be happy to prove them wrong once and for
all, and equalling his father's number of championship titles
in the very race that had taken his life seventeen years earlier
ought to do just that.

'If it were me I'd be nervous, that's all,' Sam persisted.

Maybe Tino would be too, if he stopped to think about how
he felt. But emotions got you killed in his business, and he'd
locked his away a long time ago. 'Which is why you're a cot-
tonwool lawyer in a four-thousand-dollar suit.'

'Five.'

Tino tilted his beer bottle to his lips. 'You need to get your
money back, junior.'

Sam snorted. 'You ought to talk. I think you bought that
T-shirt in high school.'

'Hey, don't knock the lucky shirt.' Tino chuckled, much
happier to be sparring with his little brother than dissecting
his current career issues.

He knew his younger brother was spooked about all the problems he'd been having that so eerily echoed his father's lead-up
to a date with eternity. Everyone in his family was. Which was
why he was staying the hell away from Melbourne until Monday, when the countdown towards race day began.

'Excuse me, but do I know you?'

Tino glanced at the blonde who had been eyeballing them
for the last ten minutes, pleasantly surprised to find her focus
on his little brother instead of himself.

Well, hell, that was a first. He knew Sam would get mileage
out of it for the next decade if he could.

He turned to see where her cute friend was but she seemed
to have disappeared.

'Not that I know of,' Sam replied to the stunner beside him, barely managing to keep his tongue in his mouth. 'I'm Sam Ventura and this is my brother Valentino.'

Tino stared at his brother. No one called him Valentino except their mother.

Switch your brain on, Samuel.

'I do know you!' she declared confidently. 'You're at Clayton Smythe—corporate litigation, L.A. office. Am I right?'

'You are at that.' Sam smiled.

'Ruby Clarkson—discrimination law, Sydney office.' She held out her hand. 'Please tell me you're in town this weekend and as free as a bird.'

Tino willed Sam not to blow his cool. The blonde had a sensational smile and a nice rack, but she was a little too bold for his tastes. His brother, however, he could see was already halfway to her bedroom.

Some sixth sense made him turn, and his eyes alighted on the friend in the black suit with the provocative red trim at the hem. She glanced at her empty table and her mouth fell open when she scanned the room and located her friend.

Then her eyes cut to his and her mouth snapped closed with frosty precision. Tino saw her spine straighten and grinned when she glanced at the door as if she was about to bolt through it. His eyes drifted over her again. If she'd bothered to smile, and he hadn't just ended a short liaison with a woman who had lied about understanding the term 'casual sex', she was exactly his type. Polished, poised and pert—all over. Pert nose, pert breasts and a pert ass. And he liked the way she moved too. Graceful. Purposeful.

As she approached, he took in the ruler-straight chestnut-coloured hair that shone under the bar lights, and skin that was perhaps the creamiest he had ever seen. His eyes travelled over a heart-shaped mouth designed with recreational activities in mind and the bluest wide-spaced eyes he'd ever seen.

'Ruby, I'm back. Let's go.'

And a voice that could stop a bushfire in its tracks.

Tino felt amused at the dichotomy; she should be leaning

in and whispering sweet nothings in his ear, not cutting her friend to the quick.

'Hey, relax. Why don't I get you a drink?' he found himself offering.

'I'm perfectly relaxed.' Her eyes could have shredded concrete as she turned them on him, but still he felt the effect of that magnificent aquamarine gaze like a punch in the gut. 'And if I wanted a drink I'd order one.'

Well, excuse the hell out of me.

'Miller!' Her friend instantly jumped in to try and ease the lash of her words. 'This is Sam and his brother Valentino. And—good news—Sam is free for the weekend.'

The woman Miller didn't move, but the skin at the outside of her mouth pulled tight. She seemed about to set her friend on fire, but then collected herself at the last minute.

'Hello, Sam. Valentino.'

He noticed he barely rated a nod.

'I'm very pleased to meet you. But unfortunately Ruby and I have to go.'

'Miller,' her friend chided. 'This is a perfect solution for you.'

This last was said almost under her breath, and Tino directed an enquiring eyebrow at Sam.

'It seems Miller needs a partner for the weekend,' Sam provided.

Tino eased back onto the barstool. *And what? They were recruiting Sam?*

He cocked his head. 'Come again?'

'No need,' the little ray of sunshine fumed politely. 'We're sorry to disturb you and now we have to go.'

'It's fine.' Sam raised his hand in a placating gesture Tino had seen him use in court. 'I'm more than pleased to offer my services.'

Services? Did he mean sexual?

Tino felt the hairs on the back of his neck stand on end. 'Would somebody like to fill me in here?' He sounded abrupt, but clearly someone had to protect his little brother from these weird females.

'Miller has to go away on a work weekend and she needs a partner to keep a nuisance client at bay,' her friend Ruby explained helpfully.

Tino eyed Miller's stiff countenance. 'Tried telling him you're not interested?' he drawled.

She snapped her startling eyes to his and once again he found himself mesmerised by their colour and the way they kicked up slightly at the corners. 'Now, why didn't I think of that?'

'Sometimes the things right in front of us are the hardest to see,' he offered.

'I was *joking*.' She looked aghast that he might have taken her sarcastic quip seriously and it made him want to laugh. It wasn't too difficult to see why she was in need of a *fake* partner, and he revised his earlier assessment of her.

She might be pert and blessed with an angel's face, but she was also waspish, uptight and controlling. Definitely not his type after all.

'Aren't you taking a client out on Dante's yacht this weekend?' He reminded his brother of the expedition both he and Dante, their older brother, had been trying to drag him along to.

Sam groaned as if he'd just been told he needed a root canal. 'Damn, I forgot.'

'Oh, really?' Ruby sounded as if she'd been given the same news.

'Okay—well, time to go,' Miller interjected baldly.

Tino wondered if she was truly thick, or just didn't want to see what was clearly going on between her friend and his brother.

'You do it.'

Tino's eyes snapped to Sam's.

'You said you were looking for something different to do this weekend. It's a great solution all round.'

Tino looked at his brother as if he had rocks in his head. His manager and the team owner had told him to take time out this

weekend and do something that would get his mind off the coming race, but he was pretty sure posing as some uptight woman's
fake partner was not what they'd had in mind.

'I don't think so,' Little Miss Sunshine scoffed, as if the very
idea was ludicrous.

Which it was.

But her snooty dismissal of him rankled. 'Have I done something to upset you?' His gaze narrowed on her face and he almost reached out to grip her chin and hold her elusive eyes
on his.

'Not at all.' But her tone was curt and her nose wrinkled
slightly when her eyes dropped to his T-shirt.

'Ah.' He exhaled. 'It's just that I'm not good enough for you.
Is that it, Sunshine?'

Her eyes flashed and he knew he'd hit the nail on the head.
He wanted to laugh. Not only had this chit of a woman not recognised him—which, okay, wasn't that strange in Australia,
given that the sport he competed in was Europe based—but
she was dismissing him out of hand because he looked a bit
scruffy. That had never happened before, and the first real smile
in months crossed his face.

'It's not that, I'm just not that desperate.'

She briefly closed her eyes when she realised her faux pas
and Tino's smile grew wider. He knew full well that if she had
recognised him she'd be pouting that sweet mouth and slipping
him her phone number instead of looking at him as if he was
about to give her a fatal disease.

'Yes, you are,' her friend chimed in.

Tino casually sipped his beer while Miller glowered.

'Ruby, *please*.'

'I can vouch for my brother,' Sam cut in. 'He looks like he
belongs on the bottom of a pond but he scrubs up all right.'

Now it was Tino's turn to scowl. He was about to say no way
in hell would he help her out when he caught her unwavering
gaze and realised that was just what she expected—was actually *hoping*—he would say, and for some reason that stopped

him. He wouldn't do it, of course. Why enter into a fake relationship when he had zero interest in the real deal? But something about her uppity attitude rattled his chain.

Before he could respond Sam continued. 'Go on, Valentino. Imagine Dee facing the same problem. Wouldn't you like some decent guy to help her out?'

Tino's glare deepened. Now, that was just underhand, reminding him of their baby sister all alone in New York City.

'It's fine,' the fire-eater said. 'This was a terrible idea. We'll be on our way and you can forget this conversation ever happened.' Her voice was authoritative. Calm. *Decisive*.

He took another swig of his beer and noticed how her eyes watched his throat as he swallowed. When they caught his again they were more indigo than aquamarine. Interesting. Or it was until he felt his own body stir in response.

'You don't think we'd make a cute couple?' He caught the wild flash of her eyes and his voice deepened. 'I do.'

Her tipsy friend was practically clapping with glee.

Miller held her gaze steady on his, almost in warning. 'No, I don't.'

'So what will you do if I don't help you out?' Tino prodded. 'Let the client have another crack at you?'

He ignored his brother's curious gaze and focused on Miller's pained expression at his crude terminology. Man, but she was wound tighter than his Ferrari at full speed, and damn if he didn't have the strangest desire to unravel her.

He tried to figure out his unexpected reaction, but then decided not to waste time thinking about it.

Why bother? He was about to send her packing with four easy words.

He threw her his trademark smile as he anticipated her horrified response. 'Okay, I'll do it.'

Miller sucked in a deep breath and gave the man in front of her a scathing once-over. He was boorish, uncouth and *dirty*—and he had the most amazing bone structure she had ever seen. He also had the most amazing grey-blue eyes surrounded by thick ebony lashes, and sensual lips that seemed to be permanently tilted into a knowing smirk. A *sexually* knowing smirk.

But clearly he was crazy.

She might need someone to pose as her current boyfriend, but she'd rather pay an escort the equivalent of her annual salary than accept *his* help. His brother would have been a different story, but no way in the world could she pretend to be interested in this man. He looked as if all he had to do was crook his index finger and a woman would come running. If she didn't swoon first.

Swoon?

Miller pulled in the ridiculous thought. The man had holes in his jeans and needed a shower, but all that aside he was far too big for her tastes. Too male.

The loud clink of a rack of freshly washed glasses brought her out of her headspace and Miller felt a flush creep up her neck as she realised she'd been staring at his mouth, and that both Ruby and Sam were waiting for her to respond.

Her eyes dropped to the man's tasteless T-shirt. Ruby must have be more affected by alcohol than Miller had realised if she seriously thought Miller would go along with this.

'Well, Sunshine? What's it to be?'

She hated his deep, *smug* tone.

About to blow him out of the water, she was choosing her rejection carefully when it struck her that he *wanted* her to say no. That he was *counting* on it.

Miller exhaled slowly, her mind spinning. The sarcastic sod had never intended to help her at all this weekend. That momentary soft-eyed look he'd got when his brother had mentioned their sister was just a ruse. The man was a charlatan and clearly needed to be brought down a peg or two. And she was in the mood to do it.

Pausing for effect, Miller steeled herself to let her eyes run over him. She was so going to enjoy watching him squirm out of this one. 'Do you happen to own a suit?' she asked sweetly.

CHAPTER TWO

Tapping her foot on the hot pavement outside her Neutral Bay apartment building, Miller again checked to see if she had any missed calls on her phone. She still couldn't believe that rather than squirm out of her phony acceptance of his help last night that thug of a man had collapsed into a full belly laugh and said he'd be delighted to help.

Delighted, my foot.

It wouldn't surprise her one bit if Valentino Ventura did a no-show on her today. He seemed the type.

Something about the way his full name rolled through her mind pinged a distant memory, but she couldn't bring it up. Maybe it was just the way it sounded. Both decadent and dangerous. Or maybe it was just the sweltering afternoon sun soaking into her black long-sleeved T-shirt combined with a sense of trepidation about this situation she had inadvertently created for herself.

She'd spent years curbing the more impetuous side of her nature after her parents had divorced and her safe world had fallen apart, but it seemed she'd have to try harder. Especially if she wanted to create a life for herself that didn't feel as precarious as the house of cards she'd grown up in.

Miller sighed. She was just tired. She'd averaged four hours' sleep a night this week and woken this morning feeling as if she hadn't slept at all.

A pair of slate-coloured eyes in a hard, impossibly handsome face had completely put her off her breakfast. As had the dream she'd woken up remembering. It had been about a man who looked horribly like the one she was waiting for, trapping her on her bed with his hands either side of her face. He'd looked at her as if she was everything he'd ever wanted in a woman and licked his beautifully carved lips before lowering his face to hers, his eyes on her mouth the whole time...

Miller's lips suddenly felt fuller, dryer, and she shivered in the afternoon heat and scanned the street for some sign of him. It must have been all those images of escorts that had set off the erotic dream, because no way could it have been about someone as reckless as she felt this man could be.

Okay. Miller gave herself a mental shakedown. She wasn't waiting around any longer for Mr Ripped Jeans to turn up. He'd had no intention of helping her out—perfectly understandable, given they were strangers and would likely never see each other again—but she couldn't fathom the tiny prick of disappointment that settled in her chest at his no-show.

Feeling silly, she shook off the sensation, frowning when a growling silver sports car shot towards the kerb in front of her and nearly rear-ended her black sedan.

About to give the owner a piece of her mind for dangerous driving, she was shocked to see her nemesis peel himself out of the driver's side of the car. She crossed her arms over her chest and puffed out a breath. He sauntered towards her, a slow grin lighting his face.

The man oozed sex and confidence, and moved with a loose limbed grace that said he owned the world. Exactly the type of man she detested.

Even though she was five foot seven, Miller wished she'd worn heels—because Valentino was nearly a foot taller and those broad shoulders just seemed to add another foot.

After her dream she had been determined to find him un-attractive, but that was proving impossible; in a white pressed T-shirt and low-riding denims, he was so beautifully male it was almost painful to look at him.

And by the shape of his biceps the man clearly spent a serious amount of time in a gym.

Fighting an urge to push back the thick sable hair that had a tendency to fall forward over his forehead in staged disarray, Miller rallied her scrambled brain and tried to conjure up a polite greeting that would set the weekend off on the right foot. Polite, appreciative and unshakably professional.

Before she could come up with something he spoke first. 'The suit's in the back. Promise.'

His deep, mocking tone had her eyes snapping back to his and she forgot all about being polite or professional.

'You're late.'

His lips curved into an easy smile as if her snarky comment hadn't even registered. 'Sorry. Traffic's a bitch at this time on a Friday.'

'You'll have to watch your language this weekend. I would never go out with a man who swore.'

His eyes sparkled in the sunlight. 'That wasn't in your little dossier.'

He was referring to the pre-prepared personal profile Ruby had insisted she hand over last night before she'd hightailed it out of the bar at the speed of light.

'I didn't think writing down that I had a preference for good manners would be necessary.'

'Seems like we'll have some things to iron out on the drive down.'

Miller bit her tongue.

Seems like?

Was he being deliberately thick-headed? His brother was a lawyer—a good one, according to Ruby—but perhaps nature had bestowed Valentino with extreme beauty and compensated by making him slow on the uptake.

'Did you fill out the questionnaire attached to my personal profile?' she asked, wishing she had checked what he did for a living.

'I wouldn't dare not.'

His humorous reply grated, and she flicked a glance at the shiny phallic symbol he was leaning against. Was it even his? 'I want to be on the Princes Highway before every other week-ender heading out of the city, so if you'd like to fetch your bag we'll get going.'

'Ever heard of the word *please*?'

The muscles in Miller's neck tightened at his casual taunt. Of course she had, and she had no idea why this man made her lose her usual cool so completely. 'Please.' She forced a smile to her lips that grew rigid as he continued to regard her without moving.

'Are you always this bossy?'

Yes, probably she was. 'I prefer the term *decisive*.'

'I'm sure you do.' He pushed off the car and towered over her. 'But here's a newsflash for you, Sunshine. I'm driving.'

Miller stared at him, hating the fact that he made her feel so small and...out of her depth. 'Is that a rental?'

'Actually, yes.' He seemed annoyingly amused by her question.

Closing her eyes briefly, Miller wondered how she had become stuck with the fake boyfriend from hell and how she was ever going to make this work.

'We're taking my car,' she said, some instinct warning her that if she gave him an inch he'd take the proverbial country mile.

He crossed his arms over his chest and his biceps bulged beneath the short sleeves of his T-shirt. Alarmingly, a tingly sensation tightened Miller's pelvic muscles, the unexpectedness of it making her feel light-headed.

'Is this our first official argument as a couple?' he asked innocently.

Okay, enough with the amusement already. 'Look, Mr Ventura, this is a serious situation and I'd appreciate it if you could treat it as such.' She could feel her heart thumping wildly in her chest and knew her face was heating up from all the animosity she couldn't contain.

Valentino cocked an eyebrow and stepped back to open the passenger side door. 'No problem, *Miss Jacobs*. Hop in.'

Miller didn't move.

'It would flay my masculinity to let a woman drive.'

Miller hated him. That was all there was to it.

Not wanting to play to his supersized ego, and feeling entirely out of her element as he regarded her through sleepy eyes, Miller made a quick decision. 'Well, I'd hate to be accused of insulting your masculinity, Mr Ventura, so by all means take the wheel.'

His slow smile told her that he'd heard her silent *shove it* and found it amusing. Found *her* amusing. And it made her blood boil.

Hating that he thought he'd won that round, she kept her voice courteous. 'As it turns out I don't mind if you drive. It will give me a chance to work on the way down.'

'But you're not impressed?'

'Not particularly.'

'What *does* impress you?'

He folded his arms across his torso and Miller's brain zeroed in on the shifting muscles and tendons under tanned skin. What had he just asked?

She cleared her throat. 'The usual. Manners. Intellect. A sense of humour—'

'You like your cars well-mannered and funny, Miss Jacobs? Interesting.'

Miller knew she must be bright red by now, and hate turned to loathing. 'This isn't funny.' She caught and held his amused gaze. 'Are you intending to sabotage my weekend?'

It gave her some satisfaction to see an annoyed look flash across his divine face.

'Sunshine, if I was going to do that I wouldn't have shown up.'

'I don't like you calling me Sunshine.'

'All couples have nicknames. I'm sure you've thought up a few for me.'

More than a few, she mused silently, and none that could be repeated in polite company.

Desperate to break the tension between them, Miller moved to the back of her car and pulled out her overnight bag. Valentino met her halfway and stowed it in the sports car before holding the passenger door wide for her.

Miller raised an eyebrow and gripped the doorframe, steeling herself to stare into his eyes. This close, the colour was amazing: streaks of silver over blue, with a darker band of grey encircling each iris.

She sucked in a deep breath and ignored his earthy male scent. 'You need to understand that I'm in charge this weekend.' Her voice wasn't very convincing even to her own ears but she continued on regardless. 'On the drive down we'll establish some ground rules, but basically all I need you to do is to follow my lead. Do you think you can do that?'

He smiled. That all-knowing grin that crinkled the outer edges of his amazing eyes. 'I'll give it my best shot. How does that sound?'

Terrible. It sounded terrible.

He leaned closer and Miller found herself sitting on butter-soft leather before she'd meant to. Her brain once again flashing a warning to run. Taking a deep breath, she ignored it and scanned the sleek interior of the car: dark and somehow predatory—like Valentino himself. It must have cost a fortune to rent, and again she wondered what he did for a living.

She couldn't look away from the way his jeans hugged his muscular thighs as she watched as he slid into the driver's seat. 'You're not a lawyer like your brother, are you?' she asked hopefully.

'Good God, no! Do I look like a lawyer?'

Not really. 'No.' She tried not to be too disappointed. 'Do you have the questionnaire I gave you?'

'No one could fault your excitement about wanting to get to know me.'

He reached into the back, his body leaning way too close to hers, and handed her the questionnaire.

Then he started the car, and Miller's senses were on such high alert that the husky growl of the engine made her want to squirm in her seat.

'You'll notice I added to it as well,' he informed her, merging into the building inner city traffic.

She glanced up, feeling completely discombobulated, and decided not to distract him by asking what he'd added. She concentrated on the questionnaire.

His favourite colour was blue, favourite food was Thai. He'd grown up in Melbourne. Hobbies: swimming, running and surfing—no wonder he looked so fit! No sign of any cerebral pursuits—no surprise there. Family: two sisters and two brothers.

'You have a big family.'

He grunted something that sounded like yes.

'Are you close?' The impetuous question was too personal, and unnecessary, but as she'd spent much of her youth longing for siblings her curiosity got the better of her.

He glanced at her briefly. 'Not particularly.'

That was a shame. Miller had always dreamed that large families were full of happy, supportive siblings who would do anything for each other.

'What does "Lives: everywhere" mean?' she asked, glancing at the questionnaire.

'I travel a lot.'

'Backpacking?'

That got a hoot of laughter. 'Sunshine, I'm thirty-three—a bit old to be a backpacker.'

He threw her a smile and Miller found her eyes riveted to his beautiful even white teeth.

'I travel for work.'

She blinked back the disturbing effect he had on her and once again scanned the questionnaire. 'Driving?' She couldn't keep the scepticism out of her voice as she read out the answer under 'Occupation'. 'Driving what?'

He threw her a quick look. 'Cars. What else?'

'I don't know. Buses? Trains?' She tried not to let her annoyance show. 'Trucks?' God, don't let him be a taxi driver; Dexter would never let her hear the end of it.

'Don't tell me you're one of those stuck-up females who only go for rich guys with white collar jobs.'

Miller sniffed. She'd been so busy working and establishing her career the last time she'd gone for any man was back at university. Not that she would be telling him that. 'Of course not.'

But she did like a man in a suit.

He snorted as if he didn't believe her, but he didn't elaborate on his answer.

Sensing he might be embarrassed about his job, she decided to let it drop for now. Maybe he wouldn't mind pretending to be an introverted actuary for the weekend. No one really knew what they did except that it involved mathematics, and not even Dexter was likely to try and engage him in that topic of conversation.

She flipped the page in front of her and found her eyes drawn to his commanding scrawl near the bottom.

Her nose wrinkled. 'I don't need to know what type of underwear you wear.' And she didn't want to imagine him in sexy boxer briefs.

'According to your little summary we've been dating for two months. I think you'd know what type of underwear I wear, wouldn't you?'

'Of course I would. But it's not relevant because I'll never need to use that information.'

He glanced at her again. 'You don't know that.'

'I could have just made something up had the need arisen.'

'Are you always this dishonest?'

Miller exhaled noisily. She was never dishonest. 'No. I loathe dishonesty. And I hate this situation. And what's more I'm sick of having men think that just because I'm single I'm available.'

'It's not just because of that?'

'No,' she agreed, thinking of TJ. 'My client isn't really attracted to me at all. He's attracted to the word *no*.'

'You think?'

'I know. It's what has made him his fortune. He's bullish, arrogant and pompous.'

'Not having met the man, I'll have to trust your judgement. But if you want my opinion your client is probably more turned on by your glossy hair, killer mouth and hourglass figure than your negative response.'

'Wha—? Hey!' Miller braced her hands on the dashboard as the car swerved around a bus like a bullet, nearly fainting before Valentino swung back into the left-hand lane two seconds before hitting a mini-van.

'Relax. I do this for a living.'

'Kill your passengers?' she said weakly.

He laughed. 'Drive.'

Miller forgot all about the near miss with an oncoming vehicle as his comments about her looks replayed in her head.

Did he really think she had a killer mouth? And why was her heart beating like a tiny trapped bird?

'I don't think we can say we met at yoga,' he said.

'Why not?' She didn't believe for a minute that he could be interested in her, but if he thought he would be getting easy sex this weekend he had another thing coming.

His amused eyes connected with hers. 'Because I don't do yoga.'

Miller felt her lips pinch together as she realised he was toying with her. 'You're enjoying this, aren't you?'

'More than I thought I would,' he agreed.

Miller released a frustrated breath. No one was going to believe she was serious about this guy. Her mother had always warned her not to lie, and she mostly lived by that creed. Yesterday, she'd let blind ambition get in the way of sound judgement.

Okay, maybe not blind ambition. Possibly she was a little peeved that she'd felt so professionally hamstrung in telling TJ Lyons what she thought of his lack of business ethics.

'Maybe we just shouldn't talk,' she muttered, half to her-self. 'I know enough.' And she was afraid if he said any more she'd ask him to pull over so she could get out and run away as fast as she could.

'I don't.'

She looked at him warily. 'Everything you need to know is in my dossier. Presuming you read it?'

'Oh, it was riveting. You enjoy running, Mexican cuisine, strawberry ice cream, and *cross-stitching*. Tell me, is that any-thing like cross-dressing?'

Miller willed herself not to blow up at him. 'No.'

'That's a relief. You also like reading and visiting art galler-ies. No mention of what type of underwear you prefer, though.'

Miller channelled the monks of *wherever*. 'Because it's ir-relevant.'

'You know mine.'

'Not by choice.' And she was trying very hard not to think about those sexy boxers under his snug-fitting jeans.

'So what *do* you prefer?'

'Sorry?'

'Are you a plain cotton or more of a lace girl?'

Miller stifled a cough. 'That's none of your business.'

'Believe me, it is. I'm not getting caught up in a conversation with your client not knowing my G-strings from my boy-legs.'

'*Potential* client. And I thought all men talked about was sport?'

'We've been known to deviate on occasion.' He threw her a mischievous grin. 'Since you won't tell me, I'll have to use my imagination.'

'Imagine away,' she said blithely, and then wished she hadn't when his eyes settled on her breasts.

'Now, there's an invitation a man doesn't get every day.'

Miller shot him a fulminating glare, alarmed to feel her nip-ples tightening inside her lace bra.

Striving to steady her nerves, she made the mistake of reading out the next item he'd added to the questionnaire. '"Favourite sexual position."'

'I haven't finished imagining your lingerie,' he complained. 'Though I'm heading towards sheer little lacy numbers over cotton. Am I right?'

Miller faked a yawn, wondering how on earth he had guessed her little secret and determined that he wouldn't know that he was getting to her. 'You've written down "all".'

He threw her a wolfish grin. 'I might have exaggerated slightly. It was getting late when I wrote that. Probably if I had to name one... Nope. I pretty much like them all equally.'

'I wasn't asking.'

'Although on top is always fun,' he continued as if she hadn't spoken. 'And there's something wicked about taking a woman from behind.'

His voice had dropped and the throaty purr slid over Miller's skin like a silken caress.

'Don't you think?'

Miller released a pent-up breath. She'd had one sexual partner so far and it hadn't been nearly exciting enough for them to try variations on the missionary theme. She hated that now all she could visualise was her on top of the sublime male next to her and how it would feel to have him behind her. *Inside her.*

Her heart thudded heavily in her chest and she suddenly found her attention riveted by the way his long fingers flexed around the steering wheel. Imagining them on her body.

'What I think is that you should concentrate on driving this beast of a car so we don't run into one of those semis you're so determined to fly past.'

'Nervous, Miller?'

He said her name as if he was tasting it and Miller's stomach clenched. Oh, this man was a master at sexual repartee, and she'd do well to remember that.

Miller shook her head. 'Are you ever serious about anything?'

He threw her a bemused look. 'Plenty. Are you ever *not* serious about anything?'

'Plenty.' Which was so blatantly untrue she half expected her nose to start growing.

He passed another car and Miller absently noted that after her earlier panicked response he was driving *marginally* less like a racing car driver. That thought triggered something in her mind and her brow furrowed.

Determined to ignore him for the rest of the trip, she pulled her laptop out of her computer bag.

'What happened to the getting-to-know-you part of our trip?'

He threw her a sexy smile that shot the hazy memory she'd been trying to grab on to out of her head and replaced it with an image of the way he had insolently leant against the bar last night.

'I know you run, swim, work out, and that you take your coffee black. Your favourite colour is blue and you have four siblings—'

'I also don't mind a cuddle after sex.'

'And you don't have a serious bone in your body. I, on the other hand, take my life very seriously and I am not interested in whether you like sex straight up or hanging from a chandelier. It's not relevant. What I'm looking for this weekend is someone to melt into the background and say very little. Starting right now.'

Tino smiled as he revved the engine and manoeuvred the Aston Martin around a tourist bus. He hadn't enjoyed himself this much in…he couldn't remember.

He was in a hot car, driving down a wide country highway on a warm spring afternoon, completely free from having to answer questions about his recent spate of accidents, his car or the coming race. The experience was almost blissful.

With any luck his anonymity would hold and he'd forget the pressure of being the world's number one racing driver on an unlucky streak. Because, as he'd told Sam, it was all media hoopla and coincidence anyway, and he'd prove it Sunday week.

He glanced at the stiff woman beside him and involuntarily adjusted his jeans. He hadn't expected her to give him a hard-on but she had. Which was surprising, given that her black linen trousers and matching shirt were about as provocative as a nun's habit.

His eyes drifted over the blade-straight hair that curtained her delicate profile from his view down over her elegant neck to the gentle swell of her breasts. Was she wearing lace underneath? By the blush that had crept into her face before he'd guess yes. The thought made him smile, and his gaze lingered on her hands as they poised over her computer keys.

She had an effortless sensuality that drew him, and whenever she glared at him hot sparks of sexual arousal threatened to burn him up.

They'd be good together. He knew it. It was just a pity he had no intention of using the weekend to test his theory.

He wasn't looking for a relationship right now, sexual or otherwise, and he had very strict guidelines about how women fitted into his life. The last thing he wanted was a woman getting into his headspace and worrying about whether or not he was going to buy it on the track every time he raced. He'd seen it too many times before, and no way would anyone land him with that kind of guilty pressure.

He still remembered the day he had watched his father clip the rear wheel of another car, flip over and slam into a concrete barrier. It had been one of those races that had reinvigorated race safety procedures and it had changed Tino's life for ever. He'd still known that he would follow in his father's footsteps, but after feeling helpless in the face of his beloved mother's grief, and fighting his own pain at losing his father, he'd locked his emotions away so tight he wasn't sure he'd recognise them any more.

Which was a bonus in a sport where emotions were considered dangerous, and his cool, roguish demeanour scared the hell out of most of his rivals.

His approach was so different from his father's attitude to the sport he'd loved. His father had tried to have it all, but what he should have done was choose family or racing. Emotional attachments and their job didn't mix. Any fool knew that.

CHAPTER THREE

'THIS it?' Valentino pulled the car onto the shoulder of the road and Miller glanced up from following the GPS navigator on her smartphone.

'Yes.' Miller read the plaque on the massive brick pillar that housed a set of enormous iron gates: 'Sunset Boulevard.' *So* typical of TJ's delusions of grandeur, Miller thought tetchily.

Valentino announced them through the security speakers, and the sports car crunched over loose gravel as he pulled around the circular driveway and stopped between an imposing front portico and a burbling fountain filled with frolicking cherubs holding gilded bows and arrows.

'Who's your client?'

Miller didn't answer. She was too busy staring at the enormous pink-tinged stone mansion that looked as if it had been airlifted directly from the Amalfi Coast in Italy and set down in the middle of this arid Australian beach scrub—lime-green lawns and all.

Her car door opened and she automatically accepted Valentino's extended hand. And regretted it. A sensation not unlike an electric shock bolted up her arm and shot sparks all the way down her legs.

Her eyes flew to his in surprise, but his expression was so blank she felt slightly stupid. At least that answered her earlier unasked question. No, he *didn't* find her attractive; he'd just been enjoying himself at her expense.

She registered the opening of a high white front door in her peripheral vision and felt her world right itself when Valentino dropped her hand.

'Miller. You made good time.'

She glanced towards her boss.

'And I can see why.' Dexter stared at Valentino and then cast his appreciative eyes over the silver bullet they'd driven down in.

A bulky figure followed Dexter down the stone steps and she pasted a confident smile on her face when TJ Lyons ambled forward like a cattle tycoon straight off the station.

'Well, now, isn't this a surprise?' he boomed.

Suddenly conscious of Valentino behind her, Miller nearly jumped out of her skin when she felt his large hand settle on her hip. Both men looked at him, eyes agog, as if he was the Dalai Lama come to pay homage.

'Dexter, TJ—this is—'

'We *know* who he is, Miller.' Dexter almost blustered, sticking his hand out towards Valentino. 'Tino Ventura. It's a pleasure. Dexter Caruthers—partner at OCG. Oracle Consultancy Group.'

Valentino took his hand in a firm handshake and a cog shifted in Miller's brain.

Tino?

'Maverick,' TJ said, addressing Valentino.

Maverick?

Had TJ and Dexter mistaken Valentino for someone they knew?

Valentino smiled and accepted their greetings like an old friend.

No! He couldn't *possibly* know her client!

'Miller, you dark horse,' TJ guffawed, slapping Valentino on the back. 'You certainly play your cards close to your chest. I'm impressed.'

Impressed? Miller looked up at Valentino, and just as her boss started asking him about the injury he'd incurred in a motor race in Germany last August his name slotted into place inside Miller's head.

Tino Ventura—international racing car legend.

She would have stumbled if Valentino hadn't tightened his hand on her hip to steady her.

She swore under her breath. Valentino must have heard it because he immediately took charge. 'It's been a long drive, gents. We'll save this conversation for dinner.'

Miller smiled through clenched teeth as he took their bags from the car and handed them to a waiting butler.

'Roger, please show our esteemed guests to their room,' TJ said, turning to the formally dressed man.

'Certainly. Sir? Madam?'

Miller refused to meet Dexter's eyes even though he was burning a hole right through her with his open curiosity.

She deliberately moved out of Valentino's reach as he went to place his hand at the small of her back. Her skin was still tingling from his earlier unexpected hold on her.

Ignoring his piercing gaze, Miller concentrated on keeping her legs steady as she preceded him up the stone steps.

Tino Ventura!

How had she not put two and two together? It was true that she didn't follow sport in any capacity, but as the only Australian driver in the most prestigious motor race in the world she should have recognised him. It was being introduced to him as Valentino that had thrown her, but even then, she conceded with an audible sigh, she'd been so stressed and distracted she might not have made the connection.

None of that, however, changed the fact that he should have told her who he was. That thought fired her temper all the way up the ornate rosewood staircase, ruining any appreciation she might have had of the priceless artworks lining the vast hall-ways of TJ's house.

Not that she cared about TJ's house. Right now she didn't care about anything but giving Valentino Ventura a piece of her mind for deceiving her.

'Stop thinking, Miller.'

Valentino's deep voice behind her sent a shiver skittering down her spine.

'You're starting to hurt *my* head.'

'This is your room, madam. Sir.'

The butler pushed open a door and Miller followed him inside. The room was spacious, and a tasteful combination of modern and old-world. At the far end was a large bay window with sweeping ocean views encompassing paper-white sand and an ocean that shifted from the brightest turquoise to a deep navy.

'Mr Lyons and his guests are about to adjourn to the rear terrace for cocktails. Dinner is to be served in half an hour.'

'Thank you.' Valentino closed the door after the departing butler. 'Okay, out with it,' he prompted, mimicking her wide-legged stance with his arms folded across his chest.

Miller stared at him for a minute but said nothing, her mind suddenly taken up by the size of the four-poster bed that dominated the large room. She glanced around for a sofa and found an antique settee, an armchair and a curved wooden bench seat inlaid into the bay window.

She heard Valentino move and her eyes followed his easy gait as he perched on the edge of the bed, testing the mattress. 'Comfy.'

He smiled, and she fumed even more because she knew he was laughing at her discomfort. 'I'm not sleeping with you in that,' she informed him shortly.

'Oh, come on, Miller. It's big enough for six people.'

Six people *her* size, maybe... Why hadn't she thought of the sleeping arrangements before now?

Probably because her mind had been too concerned with finishing her proposal and she hadn't wanted to dwell on the fact she was even in this predicament. But she *was* in it, and it was time to face it and work out how she was going to make this farce work with her fake and *very* famous boyfriend.

'It would have been nice if you had thought to let me know who you are,' she said waspishly.

'I did tell you my name. And my job.'

Miller pressed her lips together as she took in his cavalier tone and relaxed demeanour. That was true—up to a point. 'You must have known that I didn't recognise you.' She paced away from him, unable to stand still under his disturbing grey-blue gaze.

Valentino shrugged. 'If I'd thought it was going to be an issue I would have mentioned it.'

'How could you think it *wouldn't* be?' she fumed, stopping mid-pace to stare at him. 'Everyone in the country knows who you are.'

'You didn't.'

'That's because I don't follow sport, but... Oh, never mind. I need to use the bathroom and think.'

After splashing cold water on her face Miller glanced at her pale reflection and thought about what she knew about her fake boyfriend other than the garbage he'd thrown at her in the car. Taxi driver... How he would laugh if he knew she had entertained that thought for a while.

Okay, no need to rehash *that* embarrassing notion. It was time to think. Strategise.

She knew he was a world-class athlete and a world-class womaniser with a penchant for blonde model-types—although she couldn't recall where she'd read that, or how long ago. Regardless, it still made it highly improbable that they would be seeing each other. And she knew everyone who saw them together would be thinking the same thing—including Dexter, who would not be backward in asking the question.

Of course she'd refuse to answer it—she never mixed business with her personal life—but Dexter was shrewd. And he'd be too curious about her "relationship" to take it lying down. Anyone who knew her would. Serious, ambitious Miller Jacobs and international playboy Valentino Ventura a *couple*?

God, what a mess. They had as much in common as a grass-hopper with an elephant.

'You planning to hide out in there for the rest of the week-end?'

His amused voice brought her head around to stare at the closed door. Wrenching it open, she found herself momentarily breathless when she found him filling the space, one arm raised to rest across the top of the doorjamb, making him seem impossibly tall.

She pushed past him and tried to ignore the skitters of sensation that raced through her as her body brushed his. Anger. It was only anger firing her blood.

Taking a couple of calming breaths, she turned to face him. 'No one is going to believe we're a couple.'

'Why not?'

Miller rolled her eyes. 'For one, I don't exactly mix in your circles. And for two, I'm not your type and you're not mine.'

'You're a woman. I'm a man. We share a mutual attraction we can't ignore. Happens all the time.'

To him, maybe.

Miller smoothed her brows, her mind filled with an endless list of problems. 'You're right. We can't say we met at yoga…'

'Listen, you're blowing this out of proportion. Let's keep it as close to the truth as we can. We met at a bar. Liked each other. End of story. That way you'll feel more comfortable and it's highly probable—not to mention true.'

Except for the liking part. Right now Miller couldn't recall liking anyone *less*.

Valentino opened his bag on the bed.

'Why are you here?' she asked softly.

His eyes met hers. Held. 'You know why I'm here,' he said, just as softly. 'You challenged me to be here.'

Miller arched an eyebrow. 'I thought you said you were thirty-three, not thirteen.'

A crooked grin kicked up the corners of his mouth and he

pulled his shirt up over his rippling chest. Lord, did men really look that good unairbrushed?

Last night's dream flashed before her eyes and she was relieved when he turned his back on her. Only then she got to view his impressive back, and her eyes automatically followed the line of his spine indented between lean, hard muscle. 'What exactly are you doing?'

He dropped his T-shirt on the bed and turned to face her. 'Changing my shirt for dinner. I don't want to embarrass you by coming across too casual to meet your friends.'

Ha! Now that she knew who he was she knew he'd impress everyone downstairs even in a clown suit.

Tino shrugged into his shirt and tiny pinpricks of heat glanced across his back as he felt Miller's eyes on him. A powerful surge of lust and the desire to press her up against the nearest wall and explore the attraction simmering between them completely astounded him. He'd been trying to keep things light and breezy between them—his usual *modus operandi*—but his libido was insistently arguing the toss.

'Next time I'd prefer you to use the bathroom,' she said stiffly. 'And these people aren't my friends. They're business colleagues—although as to that I doubt I'll know many of the other people in attendance.'

'How many are staying here?'

'I think six others tonight. Tomorrow night at TJ's fiftieth party I have no idea.'

'I thought this was a business weekend?'

'TJ likes to multi-task.'

Tino rolled his silk shirt sleeves and noticed her frowning at his forearms. 'Problem?'

His question galvanised her into action and she crossed to her small suitcase and started rifling through it.

'I'll be ten minutes.'

Five minutes later she reappeared in the doorway and padded over to the wardrobe. She barely looked different from the way she had when she'd gone in. Black tailored pants, a black beaded top, and a thin pink belt bissecting the two. She perched on the armchair and secured a fancy pair of stilettos on her dainty feet. The silence between them was deafening.

'Am I getting the silent treatment?'

She exhaled slowly and he noticed the way the beads on her top swayed from side to side. 'I hope you're not currently in a relationship.'

'Would I be here with you if I was?'

'I don't know. Would you?'

Her chin had come up and he was surprised he had to control irritation at her deliberate slur. She didn't know him, and he supposed, given his reputation—which wasn't half as extensive as the press made out—it was a valid question.

'Okay, I'm going to humour that question with an answer—because we don't know each other and I understand you feel compromised by the fact that I'm a known personality. I don't date more than one woman at a time and I never cheat.'

'Fine. I just...' Her hand fluttered between them. 'If we really were going out you'd know I hate surprises.'

'Why is that?'

She glanced away. 'I just do.'

Her answer was clipped and he knew there was a story behind her flat tone.

'I don't suppose there's any chance you can just fade into the background and not draw attention to yourself, is there?'

Tino nearly laughed. So much for coming on to him once she found out who he was. He shook his head at his own arrogance. But, hell, most women he met simpered and preened and asked stupid questions about how many cars he owned and how fast he drove. This gorgeous female was still treating him like a disease. And she *was* gorgeous. She'd dusted her sexy mouth with a peach-coloured gloss that made him want to lick it right off.

'We need to go downstairs.' She sounded as if she was about to face a firing squad.

She grabbed a black wrap from the back of the cream chair

and stopped suddenly, nearly colliding with him. He felt a shaft of heat spear south as he touched her elbow to steady her, and knew she felt the same buzz by the way she pulled back and went all wide-eyed with shock, just as she had by the car.

A shock he himself still felt. He hadn't anticipated being this physically attracted to her. He reminded himself of his iron-clad rule of not getting involved with a woman this close to the end of the season—particularly *this* season, which had started going pear-shaped three months ago.

So why couldn't he stop imagining how she would taste if he kissed her?

He stepped back from her, out of the danger zone. 'You might want to think about not jumping six feet in the air every time I touch you.' He sounded annoyed because he was.

'And *you* might want to think about not touching me.'

Large aquamarine eyes, alight with slivers of the purest gold, stared up at him, and the ability to think flew out of his head. Her eyes reminded him of a rare jewel.

Then she blinked, breaking the spell.

Get a grip, Ventura. Since when did you start comparing eyes to jewels?

'You really have the most extraordinary eyes,' he found himself saying appreciatively. 'A little glacial right now, but extraordinary nonetheless.'

'I don't care what you think of my eyes. This isn't real so I don't need your empty compliments.'

How about the back of my hand across your tidy tush? The thought brought a low hum of pleasure winging through his body. He did his best to ignore it. 'Are you usually this rude or do I just bring out the best in you?'

Her shoulders slumped and she stepped back to put more space between them. 'I'm sorry. I'm…uncomfortable. This weekend is important to me. I wish I'd just given you chicken pox and handled everything myself. I let Ruby convince me this would be a good idea.'

Tino felt contrite at her obvious distress. 'Everything will be fine. Just think of us as two people going away for a weekend to have some fun. You've done that in the past, surely.'

'Of course,' she said, her reply a little too quick and a little too defensive. 'It's just that I would never choose to come away for a weekend with a man like you.'

He stiffened even though he knew by her tone that she was being honest rather than deliberately insulting, but, hell, he had his limits. 'What exactly is it about me that you don't like, Sunshine?' he queried, as if her answer didn't matter. Which, in the scheme of things, it didn't.

Her lips pursed at the mocking moniker, but he didn't care.

'We really need to go down.'

Tino crossed his arms. 'I'm waiting.'

'Look, I didn't mean to offend you. But I'm hardly your type either.'

'You're female, aren't you?' He couldn't help the comment. The desire to get under her skin was riding him.

'That's all it takes?'

Her incredulous tone drew a tight smile to his lips. 'What else is there?'

She shook her head. 'See, that's why you're not my type. I like someone a little more discerning, a little more…' She stopped as if she'd realised she was about to insult him.

'Don't stop now. It's just getting interesting.'

'Okay—fine. You're arrogant, condescending, and you treat everything like it's a joke.'

Tino deliberately kept his chuckle light. 'For a minute there I thought you were going to list my faults.'

She threw up her hands and stalked away from him. 'You're impossible to talk to!'

'True, but I make up for it where it counts.'

Her sexy mouth flattened and he just managed not to laugh. 'Sunshine, you are *so* easy to rile.'

She huffed out a breath and eyed him with utter disdain. 'Please remember that we are playing by my rules this weekend, not yours. When we're in company just...' She smoothed her brows. 'Just follow my lead.'

She pinned a frozen smile on her face and sailed through the door, leaving a faint trace of summertime in her wake.

Tino breathed deep. He didn't understand how a woman so intent on behaving like a man could smell so sweet. Then he wondered if she had sex like a man as well: enjoyed herself and moved on easily.

The unexpected thought made him snort as he followed her down the hall.

He might not know the answer to that, but he was damn sure they were bound to have another argument when she learned he played by no one else's rules but his own.

And as for following her lead...

CHAPTER FOUR

'So, HOW did you two meet?'

Miller swallowed the piece of succulent fish she'd been chewing for five minutes on a rush and felt it stick in her throat. It was the question of the night, it seemed, as TJ's guests tried to work out how an uptight management consultant could possibly ensnare the infamous Tino Ventura.

She grabbed her water glass and stiffened as she felt Valentino's strong fingers grip the back of her chair. He'd done that constantly throughout the meal, sometimes playing with the beads on her top, and she'd felt the heat of his touch sear through her clothing and all the way into her bones. The man was like a furnace.

Fortunately he took control of the conversation, having already warned her to say very little, but she could see he was as tired of the interest as she was.

Tuning out, she wondered if she shouldn't stage a massive fight right here and end the charade before they slipped up. Or before *she* slipped up—because he seemed to be doing just fine. And maybe she would feel better if Dexter didn't keep throwing her curious glances that told her in more than words that he didn't buy the whole international-racing-driver-boyfriend thing one bit.

When they had arrived for dinner the men had immediately enclosed Valentino in a circle as if he were an old friend, and the women had raked their eyes appreciatively over his muscular frame. Most of them had looked at him as if they wouldn't say no to being another notch on his well-scarred bedpost. Something that didn't interest Miller in the slightest.

Oh, she found him just as sexy as they did, but she had a ten-year plan that she had nearly accomplished, and she wasn't about to get involved with a man and let him distract her. Especially a man who treated women like sex bunnies.

Pushing back her chair, Miller politely extricated herself to the powder room. After locking the bathroom door she leant against it, closed her eyes and felt her heartbeat start to normalise now that she was out from under Valentino's mesmeric spell.

It didn't help that he kept touching her, and she really needed to talk to him about his ability to follow her lead. He hadn't taken *any* of her subtle hints all night. And every time he touched her—whether it was a fleeting brush of his fingers across the back of her hand at the dinner table or a more encompassing arm around her waist while sipping champagne—it made her feel as if she'd been branded.

When she had envisaged having a fake boyfriend she'd imagined someone dutifully trailing in her wake and playing a low-key, almost invisible role. But there was nothing invisible about Valentino Ventura, and it annoyed her that her own eyes were constantly drawn to him, as if he really was some god who had deigned to grace them with his presence.

Deciding she couldn't hide out in the powder room any longer, Miller exited to find Dexter lounging against the opposite wall, waiting for her.

She didn't want to think about Ruby's suspicions that Dexter was interested in her as more than just a work colleague, but there was no doubt he was behaving differently towards her all of a sudden.

'So...' Dexter drawled, a beer bottle swinging back and forth between his fingers. 'Tino Ventura?'

Miller smiled enigmatically in answer.

'You *do* know he's got a reputation for being the biggest playboy in Europe?'

She knew he *had* a reputation—but the *biggest* playboy? 'You shouldn't believe everything you read,' she said, though by the way he'd charmed everyone at dinner she could well believe it. Women were always falling for bad boy types they hoped to reform, and even clean-shaven he looked like a fallen angel.

'I don't see it, you know,' Dexter added snidely.

Miller narrowed her eyes. He might be her direct superior, but he wasn't behaving like it right now. 'My personal life is none of your business, Dexter. Was there something you wanted?'

'Your part of the presentation we're supposed to give to TJ tomorrow.'

'I e-mailed it just before I left to come down here.'

'Cutting it a bit fine?'

About to ask him what his problem was, she nearly screamed when she felt a warm male hand settle on the small of her back. She tried to quell the instant leap of her heart but it was already galloping away at a mile a minute.

She knew her reaction hadn't done anything to alleviate Dexter's scepticism about her relationship, but frankly this internal sense of excitement when Valentino came close was too unfamiliar and disconcerting to deal with head-on. She would have given anything to do what she'd done as a child in uncomfortable situations: run away to her room and lose herself in her drawings.

'Hey, Sunshine, I wondered where you'd got to.' Valentino's warm breath stirred the hair at her temple, and his gaze lingered on her mouth before lifting to hers.

He was terribly good at this, Miller thought, swallowing heavily. It was just a pity that *she* wasn't.

'Just discussing work. Nothing important,' she said breathlessly.

'In that case, you won't mind if I join you?'

'Of course not.' She smiled at Dexter, as if her world couldn't be more perfect. Anything was better than gazing up into Valentino's sleepy grey gaze.

'So, by my reckoning,' Dexter said, looking from one to the other, 'you will have met around the time of Tino's near fatality earlier in the year. In Germany. Funny, I don't recall okaying any trip to Europe in—what?—August, was it? In fact, I can't recall your last holiday at *all*, Miller.'

Near fatality?

Miller's eyes flew to Valentino's calm face and too late she realised she would of *course* know about this if they really were going out. Collecting herself, she attempted fascination with the conversation.

'Miller wasn't on holiday when we met,' Valentino answered smoothly. 'It was while I was recuperating in Australia.'

Dexter frowned theatrically. 'I thought you convalesced in Paris? Your second home town?'

'Monaco is my second home town.'

Miller noticed he hadn't directly answered Dexter's question. Clever.

'So, what do you make of your run of bad luck since your recovery?'

'It's nice to know you're such a fan, Caruthers.' Valentino's voice was smooth, but Miller felt sweat break out under her armpits.

She tried to keep her expression bland, but mild sparks of panic were shooting off in her brain. She had a vague recollection of Dexter talking sport during various meetings, but she'd had no idea he was such a motor racing fan either.

'I follow real sports.' The beer bottle swung a little too vigorously in his loose hold. 'Football, rugby, boxing,' Dexter opined.

Valentino smiled in a way that made Dexter's comment seem as childish as it was.

Undeterred, her boss tilted his head. 'And you know, of course, that Miller doesn't follow *any* type of sport.'

'Something I'm hoping to change once she sees me race in Melbourne next weekend.'

Miller felt like an extra in a bad theatre production, and

wondered why they were talking over her head as if she was some sort of possession.

'Ah, the race of the decade.' Dexter's remark was as subtle as a cattle prod.

Again, Miller had no idea what he was talking about and snuck a glance up at Valentino—to find his easy smile still in place.

'So they say.'

She could feel the tension coming off him in waves, and knew he wasn't as relaxed as he wanted them to believe. She couldn't blame him. It couldn't be easy, having Dexter grill him this way.

'You'll have to wear earplugs, Miller. It gets loud at the track,' Dexter said, valiantly trying to regain a foothold in the conversation.

'I'll take care of Miller,' Valentino drawled. 'And you'd do well not to believe everything you read on the internet, Caruthers. My private life is exactly that. Private.'

There was no mistaking the warning behind his words and Miller stared up at Valentino, slightly shocked at the ruthless edge in his tone. Gone was the dishevelled rogue who had baited her so mercilessly in the car on the drive down, and in his place was a lean, dangerous male you'd have to be stupid to take on.

And what was Dexter doing, talking about her as if they had a more personal relationship than they did?

Miller was about to take him aside and ask him but TJ chose that moment to intrude.

'There's the guest of honour!' he announced, his eyes fixed on Valentino.

Guest of honour? Since when?

Miller was starting to feel like Alice down the rabbit hole, but at least she could tell that TJ had backed off in his openly male interest in her; his awe of Valentino clearly overrode his lustful advances.

Almost ignoring her completely, TJ launched into a spiel

about his newest car on order and Miller was glad of the reprieve.

Eyes gritty with tiredness, she wished herself a hundred miles away from this scene.

Then she noticed the men looking at her and realised she'd been unwittingly drawn into a conversation she hadn't been following. Turning blindly to Valentino for assistance, she immediately became lost in his heated gaze.

Her breath stalled and she had to remind herself that this was just pretend. But, *wow*, the man could go into acting when his racing career ended and win a truckload of awards.

Hearing her phone blast Ruby's unique ringtone in her evening purse, Miller latched onto the excuse like a lifeline, not quite meeting Valentino's eyes as she slipped away from the group.

Heading straight for the softly lit Japanese garden she'd glimpsed from the dinner table, she let the subtle scent of gardenias and some other richly perfumed flower wash over her as she walked.

Tino watched Miller wander down the steps and along a rocky pathway towards the infinity pool that glowed as cobalt-blue as her eyes.

Dexter laughed at something TJ had said and Tino glanced back to find that his eyes were also on Miller. As they had been most of the night. Even a blind man could tell that they had history together. And the way her boss had tried to stamp his ownership all over her had Tino wondering if Miller hadn't needed an escort this weekend for more than just a deterrent for her avaricious client. Perhaps she needed cover for an office affair as well.

He was sure he'd heard talk about Dexter being married, and as a third generation Italian from a solid family background if there was one thing Tino didn't condone it was extramarital affairs.

His brows drew together as he considered the possibility

that Miller and Dexter were lovers, and he didn't like the feeling that settled in his gut.

Was that why she flinched every time he got within spitting distance of her? She didn't want her "real" boyfriend to get jealous? If so, she'd soon learn that he wouldn't play *that* particular game. Not for another second.

Tossing back the last of his red wine, Tino placed the glass on a nearby table before heading down the steps to the garden.

Obviously hearing his quiet footfalls on the loose pebbles, Miller turned, her face half in shadow under the warm light given off by the raised lanterns that edged the narrow path.

Tino stopped just inside the wide perimeter he'd come to recognise as her personal space and her eyes turned wary. As well they might.

'I came down here to be alone,' she said, her dainty chin sticking out at him.

Tino widened his stance. 'Are you having an affair with Caruthers?'

'What?'

She seemed genuinely appalled by the question, but she needed to know this was a boundary he wouldn't cross. 'Because if you are this little ruse is over.'

Her gorgeous eyes narrowed at his blunt comment.

'Of *course* I'm not having an affair with Dexter. But even if I was it would be none of your business.'

'Wrong, Sunshine. You made it my business this weekend.'

Miller shook her head. 'That's rubbish. You were the one who *offered* to come, and I can tell you I'm not very happy with the job you're doing so far.'

Tino felt a surge of annoyance that was as much because of his attraction to her as because of her snotty attitude. 'Want to explain that?'

She leaned in towards him and he got a whiff of her sexy scent. Unconsciously, he breathed deep. 'You agreed that you would follow my lead, but despite your silver-tongued sophistication you've failed to pick up on any of my signals.'

'Silver-ton…? Sunshine, you are deluded.'

'Excuse me?'

She mirrored his incredulous tone and Valentino didn't know whether to put her over his knee or just kiss her. The woman was driving him crazy. Or her scent was. He'd never smelt anything so subtly feminine before, and on a woman who seemed determined to hide her femininity it didn't bear thinking about. Like his unusually possessive exchange with her deadbeat boss inside.

'I never promised to follow your lead. That was an assumption you made before you so imperiously waltzed out the door. And if there's nothing going on between you and Caruthers, why is he behaving like a jealous boyfriend?'

'Why are *you*?'

'Because it's my job. Apparently. Now, answer the question.'

Her gaze turned wary again. 'I don't know what's up with Dexter except that he doesn't believe you and I are a couple.'

Tino rocked back on his heels and regarded her. 'I'm not surprised.'

She flashed him an annoyed look. 'And why is that? Because I'm not your usual type?'

Since when was a ballbreaker any man's usual type?

'Because you act like a startled mouse every time I touch you.'

'I do not,' she blustered. 'But if I do it's because I don't *want* you touching me.'

'I'm your *boyfriend*. I'm supposed to touch you.'

'Not at a business function.' She frowned.

He felt completely exasperated with her. 'Anywhere.' His voice had dropped an octave because he realised just how much he had enjoyed touching her all night. How much he wanted to touch her now.

Incredible.

'That's not me,' she said on a rush.

Her tongue snaked out to moisten her heart-shaped mouth; that succulent bottom lip was now glistening invitingly.

Valentino thrust his hands into the back pockets of his jeans and locked his eyes with hers. 'If you want people to believe we're a couple you're going to have to let me take the lead, because you clearly know diddly squat about relationships.'

She looked at him as if he'd just told her the world was about to end. '*Now* who's making assumptions? For your information, if we were in a real relationship something else you would know is that I'm not the demonstrative type.'

She had thrust her chin out in that annoyingly superior way again, and Valentino couldn't resist loading her up. 'Well, that's too bad, Miller, because if we were a real couple you'd know that I *am*.'

Which wasn't strictly true. Yes, he liked to touch, but he didn't usually feel the need to grab hold of his dates and stamp his possession all over them in public—or in private come to that. The only reason he had with Miller was because she had avoided eye contact with him most of the evening, and with all the interest in their relationship he'd had to do something to make it appear genuine.

In fact she should be *thanking* him for taking his role so seriously instead of busting his balls over it.

'Listen, lady—'

'No, *you* listen.' She stabbed a finger at him as his mother used to do when he was naughty. 'I am in charge here, and your inability to read my signals is putting this whole farce in jeopardy.'

Tino thrust a hand through his hair and glanced over his shoulder as the lilting murmur of chattering guests wafted on the slight breeze. 'Is that so?' he said softly.

'Yes.' She folded her arms. 'Trust me—I know what I'm doing.'

'Good, because right now anyone watching you spit at me like an angry cat will think we're having a humdinger of an argument.'

'That's fine with me.' She gave him a cool smile that he knew was meant to put him in his place. 'It will make our relationship seem more authentic than anything else that's gone on tonight.'

Valentino saw red at her self-righteous challenge.

He stepped farther into her personal space and gripped her elbows, gratified when her eyes widened to the size of dinner plates.

'What are you doing?' she demanded in a furious whisper.

Yeah, what are *you doing, Ventura?*

Tino stared down at her, watching the pulse-point in her neck pick up speed. His body hummed with sexual need and he wondered what it was about her he found just so damned tempting.

She was more librarian than seductress, and yet she couldn't have had more effect on his body if she'd been standing in front of him naked. It was a thought that was a little disconcerting and one he instantly pushed aside.

He wasn't *that* attracted to her. But he *was* that annoyed with her, and while he might not have ever felt the need to put a woman in her place before he did now. And he'd enjoy it.

'Why, Miller, I'm just doing what you asked. I'm going to make this farce of a relationship look more authentic.'

Before she could unload on him he took full advantage of her open mouth and planted his own firmly over the top of hers in a kiss that was more about punishment than pleasure.

Or at least it was meant to be. Until she stupidly tried to wriggle away from him and he had to clamp one hand at the back of her head and the other over her butt to hold her still.

She fell into him, her soft breasts nuzzling against his chest, her nipples already diamond-hard. They both stilled; heat and uncertainty a driving force between them. Her silky hair grazed the back of his knuckles and his fingers flexed. Her eyes slid closed, her soft whimper of surrender sending a powerful surge of lust through his whole body.

Her silky hair slid over his knuckles and made his fingers flex, and then she made a tiny sound that turned him harder than stone.

Tino couldn't have stopped his tongue from plunging in and

out of the moist sweetness of her mouth if he'd had a gun to his head. All day he'd wondered if she'd taste as good as her summery scent promised, and now he had his answer.

Better.

So much better.

He was powerless to pull back, his brain as stalled as the Mercedes he'd accidentally flooded in the second race of his professional career.

He gave a deep groan of pleasure as her arms wound around his neck, and he gripped her hips to pull her pelvis in tightly against his own.

His arousal jerked as it came into contact with her soft belly, and it was all he could do not to grind himself against her.

So much for not being that *attracted to her.*

He urged her lips to open even wider and she didn't resist when he possessed her mouth in a carnal imitation of the way his body wanted to possess hers. An instantaneous fire beat flames through his body, and her low, keening moans of pleasure were making him hotter still.

He had to have her.

Here.

Now.

His hand slid to her bottom, the outside of her thighs, drawing her in and up so that he could settle more fully in the tempting vee of her body. He felt her fingers move into his hair, her feminine curves pressing closer as she rubbed against him. Tino couldn't hold back another groan—and nearly exploded when he heard someone clearing their throat behind him.

Bloody hell. He drew his mouth back and took a moment before reaching up to unwind Miller's arms from around his neck. She made a moue of protest and slowly opened passion-drugged eyes. He knew when her senses returned from the same planet where his had gone that she'd be more than pissed.

'Sunshine, we have company,' he whispered gruffly, his unsteady breath ruffling the top of her hair.

He gave her time to compose herself before turning to face

the person behind them. He was certain it was Caruthers. He also gave himself time to get his raging hard-on under control. Not that it seemed to be responding with any speed.

Miller looked up at Valentino and was aghast to realise that she had become so completely lost in his kiss that she had quite forgotten they were in a public place.

Never before had she been kissed like that, and heat filled her cheeks at the realisation that she wouldn't have stopped if Dexter hadn't turned up. That she would have had sex with Valentino in the middle of a garden like some dumb groupie.

Not wanting to dwell on how that made her feel, Miller shoved the thought away before lurching backwards.

'Dexter…' she began, trying to organise her thoughts on the hop. She was almost glad when Valentino took over.

'You wanted something, Caruthers?'

Miller closed her eyes at Valentino's rough question and wished the ground would open up and swallow her whole.

'I came to let Miller know that TJ has opened champagne in the music room. As we're here in a professional capacity to win the man's business, it might be prudent for her to join us.'

Miller smoothed her eyebrows and stepped out from behind Valentino, determined that Dexter wouldn't see how mortified she felt right now. 'Of course.' She forced herself not to defend her actions, even though she desperately wanted to.

'Good. I'll leave you to pull yourself together,' Dexter said stiffly.

He was clearly upset with her, and he had good reason to be, Miller thought. She *was* here in a professional capacity, and even if she and Valentino really were lovers it didn't excuse her poor behaviour.

Although they *had been* secluded from the other guests, Dexter had found them—which meant anyone else could have.

A small voice informed her that Valentino had probably achieved his goal and put paid to Dexter's suspicions about the genuineness of their relationship, but Miller wasn't listening.

She wouldn't have chosen to do it that way, and she was furious that Valentino hadn't given her a choice. Furious that he had used his superior height and strength to hold her against him to prove a point. A point he had clearly enjoyed.

As did you. The snide voice popped up again, reminding her of how she had wrapped her tongue around his and tried to climb his body to assuage the ache that was still beating heavily between her thighs.

God, what a mess.

Valentino moved his arm in a gesture for her to precede him up the path and Miller determinedly made the same gesture back to him. He cocked an eyebrow at her, his eyes lingering on her mouth; his trademark sexy grin was more a warning than an indication of pleasantness.

Miller narrowed her eyes and thought about stomping on his foot as she strode past, but she decided not to give him the satisfaction of letting him know he had succeeded in rattling her again.

She knew he liked to take control but, dammit, this was not his show to orchestrate. She was in charge and it was time to set some clear boundaries between them. She'd dealt with alpha males in her line of work before, and she'd deal with this one too.

CHAPTER FIVE

FEELING as if the past hour had taken a day to pass, Miller unfolded a woollen blanket and laid it on the bedroom floor.

'What are you doing?'

She glanced up to find Valentino lounging against the bathroom doorway, watching her. His face was stony, but it only highlighted the chiselled jaw that was again in need of a razor. He wasn't wearing anything other than his black jeans, unbuttoned, and his biceps bulged where he folded his hands across his superbly naked chest.

'Problem with your shirt?' she said, and could have kicked herself when his mouth curled into a knowing smile.

'Only in as much as I don't wear a shirt to bed.'

Miller raised an unconcerned eyebrow. 'Lucky you wear jeans, then.'

'I don't.'

His eyebrow rose to match hers and she turned back to unfold a second blanket she'd picked up from the end of the bed. Flicking it out, she laid it on top of the first.

'I repeat—what are you doing?'

'Making up a bed. What does it look like?'

Valentino looked bored. 'If you're worried about whether or not I'm going to jump your bones now that we're alone, I doubt I could get through that passion killer you're wearing with a blowtorch.'

Miller stood up and moved to the wardrobe, where she had seen a group of pillows on the top shelf. She was glad that he didn't like her quilt-style dressing gown. It had been a present from her late father, and although the stitching was frayed in places she'd never get rid of it.

Thinking about her father made her remember the day her parents had told her they were separating. She'd been ten at the time, and while they'd talked about it calmly and rationally Miller had felt sick and confused. Then her mother had driven her from Queensland to Victoria and Miller's world had gone from cosy and safe to unpredictable and unhappy. A bit like the steely, coiled man feigning nonchalance in the bathroom doorway.

'Or are you worried you won't be able to keep your hands to yourself after that kiss?' he asked.

Miller cast him a withering look and returned to the bed she was setting up on the floor. She wasn't going to stroke his ego by responding to his provocative comments.

He'd felt her response to his kiss and it still rankled. Afterwards she'd pretended that she'd been acting for the sake of their audience, but she hadn't been, and she needed time to process that.

In the space of a short time the solid foundations of her secure life had become decidedly rickety, and she wasn't going to add to that by letting her plans for the future be derailed by a sexy-as-sin flamboyant racing car driver who treated life like a game. Because Miller knew life *wasn't* a game, and when things went wrong you only had yourself to rely on.

It had been a tough lesson she had learned hard after being sent to an exclusive girls' boarding school, where her opinion hadn't meant half as much as her lack of money. Teenage girls could be cruel, but Miller hadn't wanted to upset her mother by telling her she was having a terrible time at school. Her mother had needed to work two jobs in order to give Miller a better start in life than she'd had, so Miller had put up with the bullying and the loneliness and made sure not to give her mother any reason to be disappointed in her.

'If you think I'm sleeping on that, Sunshine, you're mistaken.'

Valentino's arrogant assurance was astounding, and Miller stared open-mouthed as he crossed to the bed and placed his watch on the bedside table.

Fortunately she had already anticipated this problem and, she thought grumpily as she fluffed up her pillows, she hoped the bed had bugs in it.

'Good to know. At least there won't be any more arguments between us tonight.'

Tino smiled. He couldn't help it. Which was surprising since he was still irritated as hell by that kiss out in the garden and the way he had become completely lost in it. Drunk on it.

He'd told himself all day to lay off the little fantasies he'd been having about her mouth, but had he listened? No.

And what was up with that? If he ignored his instincts on the track as he had out in that garden he'd have bought the farm a long time ago.

The problem was he had made her off-limits and that had spiked his interest. Stupid. But he wasn't a man who could resist a challenge. And on top of that she was clearly not fawning over him as other women did once they knew who he was. There was nothing more likely to get a woman into his bed than giving them his job title, but this pretty little ray of sunshine was not only *not* trying to sleep with him, she was making up a bed on the floor!

She couldn't have challenged him more if she'd tried, and because he had been thwarted in racing these last couple of months, first due to injury and then because his car was under-performing and causing all sorts of problems, he was more frustrated than he normally would be. Which went a lot further towards explaining his sexual fascination with her than anything else he'd come up with so far.

It was even more of a reason to keep his distance from her.

He wasn't a slave to his hormones, and he had enough complications at the moment without adding her to the list.

He yanked off his jeans and got into the king-sized bed, letting out an exaggerated sigh of appreciation as the soft mattress gave just enough beneath his body. He might as well enjoy it since he *knew* she was about to order him to sleep on the floor. He'd do it once she said please. A word she was sorely in need of learning how to use.

He grinned. He was quite looking forward to seeing how long it would take before she caved in and used it.

He watched with some satisfaction as she stalked to the main door and hit the light switch with her open palm as if she wished it was his head. Then she did something completely unexpected. She shimmied out of her robe and got into the makeshift bed on the floor.

And made him feel like an absolute idiot.

'Ever had your testosterone levels checked out?' he grumbled.

'What's the matter, Valentino? Your masculinity being challenged because I'm not falling at your feet?'

Yes, as a matter of fact it was.

'Was the kiss that good?' he purred.

'I can't remember.'

He heard her fake a yawn and shook his head. 'Sounds like you want a reminder.'

'Not in this lifetime,' she sputtered.

Her protest was a little too vigorous, which he liked.

Tino stretched out on the bed and stared at the ceiling, his eyes starting to adjust to the grey shadows cast around the room from the moonlight seeping in around the sheer curtains.

He heard the blankets on the floor rustle and his teeth gnashed together. She was being ridiculous and taking this just a little too far. He wondered if she was wearing something lacy. Something like the freshly laundered hot-pink thong hanging on the towel rail in the bathroom. The sight of those delicate panties had knocked him for a six, and he was pretty sure she hadn't left them there deliberately.

Finding out she really *did* favour sexy lingerie was a fact he could have well done without. Ball-breaking Miss Miller Jacobs was turning out to be full of contradictions. Not least of all that fiery response to his kiss in the garden.

Acting, she had said after the event. *Yeah, right.*

Acting, my ass.

Yeah, and you're not supposed to be thinking about it.

'I like the thong you left in the bathroom,' he said, unable to help annoying her as she was annoying him.

'You can't borrow it,' she said after a slight pause.

He gave a soft chuckle. *Man*, she was sassy. And, no, he didn't want to borrow it. But he wouldn't have minded stripping it down her long legs to see what he was sure would be tawny curls underneath. His heart beat the blood a little more heavily around his body and he was unable to stop his mind from imagining her naked and spread out on the four-poster bed. Imagining her soft and wet with the same need that had compelled her to wrap her tongue around his in that garden.

He breathed deep and willed his body to relax, reminding himself that he only wanted her because he'd placed an embargo around her.

The blankets rustled again as she adjusted herself on the hard floor that not even thousand-dollar-a-metre carpet could soften.

His blood was Sicilian, and if she thought he could stay sprawled out on a comfortable bed while she lay uncomfortably at his feet she had another thing coming. But he knew offering up the bed would only play into her martyr's hands and give her a reason to make him feel even more like a heel, so he stayed quiet and devised another plan that had the double advantage of allowing him to live up to his chivalrous nature and annoy the hell out of her at the same time.

Half an hour later Tino looked down on Miller's sleeping form. Her hands were tucked under her face and her shoulder-length hair was dark against the white pillow. Deep shadows beneath her eyes attested to how tired she was.

Careful not to wake her, he leaned down and pulled the meagre blanket away from her body—and instantly stilled.

She was lying half on her stomach, one leg bent to the side in an innocently provocative pose. Her pale jersey camisole top and matching three quarter length pants stretched tight over her ripe curves. As far as night attire went it wasn't the most seductive he'd ever seen, and yet as he gazed at her slender limbs, milky in the shadowy moonlight she had his full attention.

His hand itched to curve around the firm globes of her bottom while he bit down gently on the soft-as-silk skin that covered her trapezius. Would she be sensitive there? Or would she prefer him to kiss his way down each pearl-like button of her spine? Perhaps while he was buried deep inside her.

Tino groaned and closed his eyes. He felt like a randy teenager looking at a full on girlie magazine. Lust, hot and primal, beat through his body and made his legs weak. For a moment he was gripped by an almost uncontrollable urge to roll her over and wake her with a lover's kiss. Get her to open her mouth for him as she had done earlier, cup her pert breasts, shove those stretchy pants to her ankles and thrust into her until all she could do was chant his name over and over as she came for him.

Only him.

He blinked back the unusually possessive thought, the incongruity of it burning through his sensual haze and reminding him of his initial purpose in pulling the blanket from her body.

Gently, he scooped her up off the floor and carried her to the bed. She stirred and shifted in his arms, the curtain of her hair trailing down his naked arm and her orange blossom shampoo tickling his nose. His body tightened at the allure of that clean smell and he almost tumbled her onto the bed in his haste to put her down. As soon as he did she mumbled something unintelligible and sighed deeply as she curled into the soft mattress.

Tino quickly pulled the comforter up over her near naked limbs before he could change his mind about being chivalrous.

His eyes drifted to the other side of the king-sized bed. It looked vast and empty with her only taking up one quarter of it. Tiredness invaded his body, and although he had fully intended to sleep on the floor he realised he probably didn't have to. The bed was nearly as big as the infinity pool downstairs and he was an early riser. If the gods were on his side he'd be up and running along the beach before she even knew it was a new day.

Still, he laid a row of pillows down the centre of the bed. No point in tempting fate.

'Oh, yes,' Miller moaned softly as she felt the weight of a hair roughened thigh slip between her legs while a warm, callused hand palmed her breast. Her body buzzed and her nipples tightened, forcing her to arch more firmly into that warm caress. The hand squeezed her gently and somewhere above her head she heard a rough masculine sound of appreciation. Another hand was sliding confidently over her hip toward—

Holy hell!

Miller's eyes flew open and she stared straight into Valentino Ventura's sleeping face. Within seconds her brain assimilated the fact that she was no longer on the floor, but in bed and that Valentino had one of his hands on her breast and the other curved around her bottom.

Miller yelped and pushed against his impossibly hard chest, glad when he gave a grunt of discomfort, his jet-black lashes parting to reveal slate-grey eyes still glazed with sleep.

Miller pushed at his hands and scrambled backwards, her legs colliding with one of his knees as she roughly slid her leg out from between his.

Tino let out a rough expletive and moved his legs out of the way. 'Watch the knee.'

'Watch the...?' Miller had a vague recollection of the men questioning Valentino about some racing injury but she didn't care about that right now. 'Get your hands off me, you great oaf.'

She shoved harder at his immovable arm and sucked in

her tummy muscles as his steely forearm slid across her bare stomach.

Finally, fully awake, he acquiesced.

'No need to sound the alarm, I was just sleeping.'

Miller gripped the duvet up to her chin. 'You were groping me.'

'Was I? I thought you'd just ruined a pleasant dream. Sorry about that.'

'Yes, I just bet you're sorry.' She saw his eyes sharpen on hers. 'How did I end up in bed with you anyway?'

Valentino casually slid his hands beneath his head and Miller swept her angry gaze over those powerful arms and that muscular chest. She felt her breath catch and her heartbeat speed up and berated her instant reaction.

'I don't know, Sunshine,' he answered. 'Are you prone to sleepwalking?'

Miller narrowed her gaze, her mind flashing back to last night. A vague memory of being lifted floated to the surface of her mind. 'You carried me.'

Valentino yawned and pushed up until he was leaning against the headboard. The sheet dropped down to his waist, and the morning sun fell over part of his bronzed chest and corrugated abdomen as if lighting him up for a photo shoot.

He scratched his chest and her eyes soaked him up. God, the man really did look airbrushed!

'Damn. Maybe *I'm* prone to sleepwalking,' he said.

Miller hugged the duvet closer and felt her nipples throb with awareness as her hands accidentally grazed over them. Heat immediately bloomed in her face at the memory of *why* her breasts felt so heavy and sensitive.

'This isn't funny. That's sexual harassment.'

The great oaf just rolled his eyes. 'As I recall it, it was you who cuddled up to me in your sleep—not the other way around.'

'I did not.'

'Suit yourself. But last night I put a row of pillows between us, and I know it wasn't *me* who knocked them aside. Anyway,

I disengaged my hand as soon as you asked.' He raised and lowered his knee gingerly beneath the blanket and she hoped that she *had* hurt him.

'Remind me not to do you a good deed again,' he said.

'Ha. Good deed, my foot. You wanted to…to…'

'Have my wicked way with you?' His eyes glinted. 'If that was what I wanted that's what we'd be doing.'

'You wish.'

'A challenge, Miller?'

She didn't deign to respond. Why would she? Of course it wasn't a challenge—especially when she had liked the feel of him against her a little too much.

Her breathless response reminded her of the time she'd been secretly trapped in the girls' toilets at the hideous school she'd attended while the main bullies had loitered, giggling vacuously over some boy or another.

By the time they had hit fifteen, boys had been all they could talk about. Miller had wanted to yell, *What about when it all goes wrong?* But of course she hadn't. She hadn't wanted to look more like a freak than they already thought she was. All of them had seemed content to live in the moment in a way she never could after her parents had divorced.

'There was no way I was letting you sleep on the floor. Get over it.' Valentino's gruff voice jolted her back to the present.

'Turn the other way,' she demanded, letting her painful memories slip away.

When he complied without argument she shot out of bed and snatched up her robe. Ignoring him, she grabbed her running clothes and stalked towards the bathroom.

'Just so we're clear.' She stopped in the doorway. 'This arrangement does *not* extend to sex, and even if it did you would be the last man I would choose to sleep with.'

He looked at her as if he could see right through her. 'So you keep saying.'

His intense eyes never left hers and Miller found it hard to swallow. He looked irresistible and dangerous with his untidy dark hair and overnight stubble. By contrast she was sure she looked a fright, and all of sudden it seemed imperative that she get away from him. She couldn't remember ever feeling so vulnerable.

She shook her head. 'You're too used to getting your own way. That's your problem.'

Valentino threw back the covers and stood up. He was only wearing low-riding hipster briefs and Miller quickly averted her eyes. She felt irrationally angry when he laughed. He stalked towards her and Miller deliberately held his gaze, refusing to let him see how affected she was by his potent masculinity.

He shook his head. 'Lady, you are one overwound broad. Yes, my hand was on your breast—but that little moan you exhaled before your uptight brain kicked into gear let me know that you liked it. More than liked it.'

'Well, my uptight little brain rules my body, and what you felt back there was just a physiological reaction.' Miller felt irrationally stung by his assessment, even though she had insulted him first. She couldn't help it; he just made her feel so… so…*emotional*!

'You're telling me you'd get turned on if you woke up with TJ's hand on your breast?'

Miller clamped her lips together. That was a no-win question and they both knew it. 'There's no way to answer that without stroking your mountainous ego, so I won't bother.'

'You just did.'

Oh! Miller swivelled and slammed the bathroom door in his laughing face. He was *so* arrogant and *so* full of himself.

Impossible. The most impossible and most gorgeous man she had ever come across.

She leant back against the door and sighed. No wonder he had women lining up outside his hotel rooms to get a glimpse of him. The man was sex on legs and he knew it.

Miller made a frustrated noise through her teeth and her breasts tingled with remembered pleasure as she pulled on her shorts, sports bra and top. A strenuous run would help her forget this morning before her meeting with Dexter and TJ.

Taking a fortifying breath, she decided to ignore Valentino—but that plan instantly unravelled when she opened the bathroom door and noticed him sitting on the side of the bed, tying his shoelaces and dressed as she was.

'Please tell me you're not going for a run?'

Valentino looked up. 'Is there a law against it?'

His eyes immediately dropped to her bare legs and Miller felt slightly uncoordinated as she continued across the room to the closet.

She wanted to say yes, but he would no doubt think she was being uptight again—and anyway it was petty. The man was doing her a favour by being here—albeit a reluctant one—and who was she to tell him he couldn't go for a run? She might dislike the tumultuous feelings he incited in her just from looking at him, but she was going to have to get used to it if she was going to survive the next twenty-four hours with any degree of dignity. She had already decided she wasn't going to be his weekend plaything, so how hard could it be?

'Of course not,' she said, knowing full well he was a hundred times fitter than she was and would never suggest they run together.

'You run often?' he asked.

Miller glanced his way, noting his conciliatory tone. 'A couple of times a week. You?' she added, deciding to accept his olive branch.

'Every morning except Sunday.'

She didn't want to ask what he did on Sunday mornings. She was afraid her hormones would want her to do more than just visualise it.

He tilted his head, that devilish smile playing around his lips. 'I get time off for good behaviour.'

The incongruity of that statement brought an instant grin to her face. 'Yeah, right. I'm sure you were the type of teenager who crawled out of your bedroom window when your parents were asleep and partied all night.'

'They were called study nights at our house.' His deadpan expression made her laugh.

When she realised that he was laughing too she quickly sobered. Because she didn't want to enjoy his company, and by the wary darkening of his eyes he didn't much want to enjoy hers either.

But still the light-hearted connection persisted and made her nervous. A sudden impulse to place his hand back on her breast and kiss him senseless blindsided her.

'It's a beautiful morning. Why don't we stretch on the beach first?' he suggested.

Shocked by the unfamiliar emotions driving her thoughts and desperate to break the tension that throbbed between them, Miller cleared her throat and hoped that single gesture hadn't transmitted to him just how affected she was by his presence.

'I don't think we should run together.'

Valentino eyed her dubiously. 'How will it look if you run off in one direction and I go in the other?'

Telling, probably.

Miller smoothed her eyebrows in a soothing gesture that failed dismally.

She looked down at his long muscular legs dusted with dark hair.

'Come on, Miller, what are you afraid of?'

Him, for one. Her own feelings, for two. Did he need three? 'I'll slow you down,' she mumbled.

'I'll forgive you,' he replied softly.

Miller sighed. One of her strengths was knowing when she was beaten, but still she was hardly gracious when she said. 'Okay, but don't talk to me. I hate people who run and talk at the same time.'

CHAPTER SIX

THE morning *was* beautiful. Peaceful. The air was crisp, but already warmed by the sun beating down from a royal-blue sky, and the fresh scent of saltwater was tart on the silky breeze. Seagulls flew in graceful circles, while others just squatted on the white-gold sand, unaffected by the gentle, almost lackadaisical nature of the waves sweeping towards them.

The beach arced around in a gentle curve towards a rocky outcrop, and as it was in an unpopulated area it was completely deserted at this time of the morning.

After a few quick stretches Miller set off at an easy jog along the dark, wet packed sand left behind as the tide went out, sure that Valentino would get bored and surge ahead. But he didn't. And then she remembered that he'd complained about his knee and wondered if she *had* hurt him this morning.

Feeling hot already, Miller turned her head to look at him, her ponytail swinging around her face. 'I didn't really hurt your knee, did I?' she panted between breaths.

He glanced across at her, only a light sheen of sweat lining his brow, his breathing seemingly unaffected by his exertions. 'No. The knee is fine.'

'Was the accident very bad?'

When he didn't respond, she flicked her eyes over his profile, just in time to see him tense almost imperceptibly.

'Which one?'

'There's been more than one?'

He glanced towards the ocean, and she didn't think he'd answer.

'Three this year.'

She wasn't sure if that was a lot for his profession. She imagined they must crash all the time at the speeds they drove. 'The one where you hurt your knee?'

He didn't look at her. 'Bad enough.'

His voice was gruff, blunt. Very unlike his usual casual eloquence. 'Was anyone else hurt?'

'Yes.'

'Wh—?'

'I thought you said you didn't like to talk while you ran?'

It was pretty clear he didn't want to tell her about it so she let the subject drop. But of course her curiosity was piqued. Dexter's comment about his next race being the race of the decade was making her wonder if it had anything to do with his accident. She really didn't know anything about Valentino Ventura, other than the fact that he was called Maverick and he dated legions of women, but she wouldn't mind knowing what secrets she was beginning to suspect lay behind his devil-may-care attitude to life.

Tino had never run with anyone before. Not even his personal trainer. Running was meditative, and something he liked to do alone, so he hadn't expected to enjoy Miller's company as much as he was.

Despite his large family he wasn't the type to need others to be close to him. He was a loner. Maybe not always, but certainly since his father's death. And, yeah, he knew a shrink would say the two were connected but he was happy with the way he was and saw no reason to change. If he died one day pushing the limits, as his father had, and Hamilton Jones had last August, at least he knew he wouldn't be leaving a devastated family behind him.

The image of Hamilton's wife and two young daughters—

teary and slightly accusing at the funeral, because he'd survived and their father hadn't—caused guilt to fluctuate inside him.

Survivor guilt.

The team doctor had warned him about it afterwards, and while he'd never admitted to feeling it he knew that on some level he did. But he also knew it was something that would wear off if he didn't think about it. Because the accident hadn't been his fault. Hamilton had tried to overtake on one of the easiest corners on the track, but had somehow managed to clip Tino's rear wheel and hurtle them both out of control.

Hamilton had lost his life and Tino had missed three of the following races due to injury. And he'd failed to finish the last two races due to mechanical issues.

He wasn't superstitious, and he didn't believe in bad luck, but he couldn't deny—at least to himself—that there seemed to be a black cloud, like in a damned cartoon strip, following him around at the moment.

A sudden memory of the moment his mother had returned from the bathroom and he'd had to tell her that his father—the love of her life—had just been involved in a hideous accident clamped around his heart like an iron fist. No one knew what had caused the accident that had ended his father's life—engine malfunction or human error—but the pit crew had said his father hadn't been himself that morning, and Tino remembered overhearing his mother urge his father to pull out of the race. But the old man had ignored her and gone anyway.

Tino swiped a hand through his hair. Had that been what had killed him? His mother's soft request? Tino shuddered. It was a hell of a position for a man to be put in.

Refocusing on Miller's steady rhythm, he was surprised that he didn't have to temper his speed all that much for them to remain together.

Waking up beside her, he hadn't meant to have his hands all over her, and now he decided that it would be best to play the relationship game her way. So what if Caruthers had the hots for her? It was none of his business, as she had rightly pointed out. Now that he knew he wasn't being used as a patsy to hide an affair it shouldn't mean anything to him that the other man wanted her.

Had they *ever* been lovers?

Not wanting to head down that particular track he concentrated again on the rhythmic sound of their feet hitting the sand and the crystal clear waters of the South Pacific Ocean rolling onto the beach. The coastline reminded him a little of his house on Phillip Island, near Melbourne, although he knew the water there was at least ten degrees cooler and a hundred times rougher.

Miller stopped and started walking, her hands on her hips, and Valentino joined her.

'You can keep going if you want,' she panted.

He glanced at her. He *could* keep going but he didn't want to. What he wanted was to stop thinking about the past and make her smile. Like she had back in their room. He wondered what she did for fun, and then wondered why he cared.

'You work out a lot?' he asked.

She glanced at him, and he tensed when her eyes dropped to his stomach as he used his T-shirt to wipe a line of sweat off his brow. He knew she was attracted to him, maybe even as attracted as he was to her, but he also knew it would be stupid to follow up on that attraction. Not only did *she* not want it—he didn't either. And, while his body might have ideas to the contrary, his body was just an instrument for his mind, not the other way around.

'I go to the gym three times a week and try to go for a run along the Manly foreshore on the weekend.'

She walked in a small circle to ease the lactic acid burn from her legs.

'You do weights?'

'Some. Mainly light weights. Although I missed every one of my workouts this week due to work, so no doubt when I start back Monday morning I'll be a little sore.'

'Do some now.'

She cast her eyes from the sparkling ocean to the sand dunes behind them. 'I'm sorry, but if you see a weight machine anywhere around here you're on your own.'

He laughed. 'There's a lot you can do without machines. Trust me. This is part of my day job. Why don't we start with some ab crunches?'

He lay on his back and started curling his head towards his bent knees. He'd made it to twenty when out of the corner of his eye he saw her reluctantly join him. He wasn't sure why that pleased him so much.

She kept pace for a minute, then fell back on the sand. 'I've been running for a while but I'm still pretty new at the gym thing,' she said.

'Okay, now squats.'

Miller groaned. 'I really don't like squats.'

'No one likes squats except bodybuilders.'

She laughed and the husky sound made his stomach grip.

'Come on.' His voice was gruff, unnatural sounding.

She jumped lithely to her feet and he couldn't look away from the toned muscles in her thighs as she braced her legs slightly apart.

'Raise your arms overhead as you go down. And keep your chest up.' He cleared his throat, trying to concentrate on her technique rather than recalling the feel of her peaked nipple pressing eagerly into his palm. 'Squeeze your glutes and extend through your hips as you come up.'

He'd need to dunk himself in the ocean at this rate, but at least his mind was fully focused on something other than racing again.

'Am I getting a personal training session now?' She grinned at him, but didn't stop.

'Maybe.' He returned her smile. 'I do aim to please.'

'What's next?' She breathed deep and shook out her legs.

Tino could think of a lot of 'nexts' that involved her horizontal on the soft sand without the top and shorts, but he shouldn't even be thinking like that.

He sucked in a litre of air and took her through a couple of other light exercises. 'Push-ups.'

Miller grimaced. 'Oh, great. You're hitting all my favourites.'

She got down on the sand and started pushing herself up, her knees bent.

'They're not real push-ups,' he teased.

'Yes, they are!' After twenty she collapsed and rolled onto her back. 'Okay, that's it. Those and the bench press are my weakest exercises.'

He absently noted how the sun had turned her hair to burnished copper, with some of the tendrils around her temples darkened with sweat. Her cheeks were pink from exertion, her chest heaving...

Don't even go there, Ventura.

'That just means you have to do more of them.'

Miller turned her head towards him and her eyes sparkled as blue as the ocean behind her. 'Oh, darn. No bench press. What a shame.'

Tino smiled. So she did have a sense of humour.

Lifting from his sitting position beside her, he came over the top of her, before he could talk himself out of it, his body hovering far too close to her own.

Her eyes flew wide and her hands fluttered between them, the pulse-point at the base of her throat hammering wildly. 'Valentino, what are you doing?'

He liked the way she used the full version of his name. Breathless. Husky.

'Accommodating you.' His own voice was rough again, as if he'd swallowed a mouthful of sand, and he hoped to hell she hadn't noticed that he was already fully hard. 'I'll be your bench press.'

'Don't be silly.'

He braced himself on his arms and lowered his upper body slightly over hers. 'Hands on my shoulders,' he commanded.

When she put them there he barely suppressed the shudder that ran the length of his whole body.

She shifted beneath him. Swallowed. 'This won't work,' she said, but she didn't remove her hands. 'You're too big.'

Her eyes met his and the air between them sizzled.

She was wrong. This wasn't silly. This was way beyond silly. 'Ten reps. Go.' He just wanted them out of the way now.

She pushed at his shoulders and he mentally worked his way through every component of a car engine as they moved in unison. He could feel her hot breath on his neck as she exhaled and he dared not look at anything but the sand above her head.

Of all the lame-brain things to do...

He paused when he felt her weaken, intent on pushing himself away from her, but he made the mistake of looking down into eyes that had gone indigo with desire.

The sound of seagulls squalling couldn't even distract him from the hunger that burned a hole in his belly.

Her hands slipped down his arms, shaping his muscles, and her eyes drifted to his mouth. 'Valentino...'

Her husky plea weakened him more than fifty reps with twenty-five-pound dumbbells could and, groaning deep in his chest, he lowered his head and captured her soft mouth with his own.

Miller was aware of every hard inch of Valentino's male flesh pressing her into the sand. Her own body throbbing as if it was on fire, totally drugged by his heat, his smell, his taste. She couldn't remember why this was a bad idea. No rational words remained in her head to rein in her pleasure-fuelled body. Her arousal with him in bed earlier had returned full-force.

Impatient with a need she'd never felt before, she swept her hands down his back and then smoothed them up under his sweaty shirt. He groaned approvingly and with his elbows either side of her face cradled the back of her head, angling her so that his skilful mouth could ravage her lips, his moist tongue plundering and duelling with her own in a way that made the ache between her legs become almost painful.

She felt his other hand drift over her torso, feather-light as if learning her shape, his fingertips moving closer and closer to the tip of one breast. Moaning, Miller twisted in his hold, her body begging for more of his touch. She felt him smile against her mouth, his lips drifting over her jaw and down the column of her throat.

'Please, Valentino...' she pleaded, her body craving a release she had never experienced during sex but which now seemed infinitely possible. Infinitely desirable.

Obliging her, his hand rose over her breast, cupping her, his thumb flicking back and forth over her nipple at the same time as his teeth bit down on the straining, sensitive cord of her neck.

Miller cried out, jerking beneath him. Her body was liquid with need, her hips arching towards his, her mind completely focused on one outcome.

His fingers plucked more firmly at her nipple and her fingernails unconsciously scored the tight muscles of his lower back.

He shifted sideways and she whimpered in protest. Then his hand slid lower, and she stopped breathing as he cupped between her legs.

'Miller—'

She didn't want him to speak. She just wanted to lose herself in these magic sensations. She dragged his mouth back to hers, her tongue instantly gratified by the warm wetness of his deep, soul-destroying kiss. Her body was close, so close, and she couldn't think, couldn't breathe.

'Oh!'

His hand slipped beneath the hem of her shorts and knickers and then his fingers parted her and lightly stroked her swollen flesh. He groaned into her mouth, pressed deep at the same time as Miller pressed upwards, and that was all it took for her to tumble over the edge. She gripped his shoulders and wrenched her mouth from his, gasping for oxygen as her body disintegrated into a million wonderful pieces.

For a while nothing happened, and then she became aware of the sound of Valentino's harsh breathing above her own panting breaths, the seagulls squalling overhead.

When she finally managed to open her eyes she found him looking down at her with an open hunger that made her feel instantly panicked.

Oh, God... 'What have I done?'

'I believe it's called having an orgasm,' he mocked, clearly understanding the horrified expression on her face. 'Followed closely by feeling regret.'

Regret? *Did* she regret it? She didn't even know. But all the reasons this was not a good idea rushed back like a blast of cold water from a hose.

Public beach. Playboy. Promotion.

If she could bury her head in the sand right now she would.

A seagull squawked close by and Miller jumped. 'You have to get off me.'

'I'm not actually on you.'

He was right. His body hovered beside her, shielding her from any prying eyes at TJ's house some way along the beach, but he wasn't holding her down.

Miller scrambled to a sitting position and looked over his shoulder. They were still alone. Thank God.

'I said I wasn't going to have sex with you,' she spat at him accusingly. She knew full well that she was equally responsible for what had just happened between them, but was still unable to fully take in the sensations rippling through her body. 'This never happened,' she said firmly, her emotions as brittle as an empty seashell.

His eyebrows drew together and his features were taut. 'Not part of your plan, Sunshine?'

'You know it wasn't.' She hated the sarcastic tilt to his lips.

'Believe me, it's not part of mine either.' He pushed himself to a sitting position and deftly removed his runners and socks. Then he dragged his T-shirt up over his chest and Miller's insides, still soft and pliant, clenched alarmingly.

His easy acceptance of her brush-off was slightly insulting, and the illogical nature of that thought wasn't lost on her in the heat of the moment. In fact, it only made her more irritable. But whether at him or herself she wasn't sure.

She watched him jog down to the shoreline and gracefully duck dive beneath an incoming wave. Thank God she didn't like him very much. She wasn't ready to change her life for a man, and some deep feminine instinct warned her that being with him intimately, even once, would be life-changing.

She sighed. At least for her it would be. For him life would no doubt go on as normal.

CHAPTER SEVEN

TJ TIPPED his Akubra back from his forehead and rocked forward on his chair, and Miller knew the presentation she and Dexter had just delivered hadn't gone well.

'Miller, you're a talented girl, no doubt about it,' he drawled, in a condescending tone that set Miller's teeth on edge. 'But I told Winston International I'd give their show another shot.'

What?

Miller narrowed her eyes, sensing Dexter's surprise without having to look at him.

The reason TJ had even approached Oracle was because he was disgruntled with the service he'd been receiving from Winston International.

'I was thinking about it all last night, and it doesn't seem right to trash our relationship after so many years. One of their boys is going to show me what they've got Monday morning. In the meantime why don't you fix the concerns I have with your current proposal and get it back to me ASAP?'

Miller was thankful for the years of practice she'd had at pretending she was perfectly fine when she wasn't, and schooled her features into an expression of professional blandness. Was this because she'd rejected his advances in the restaurant the week before? He might be ruthless and without morals, but he didn't strike her as the vindictive type. But he did know Oracle *was* desperate for his business, so he had them over a barrel in that regard.

She had started to hate this aspect of business. The 'anything goes' mantra Oracle had adopted as the global economic crisis had deepened. In some ways she supposed it had always been there, but she hadn't noticed it in her single-minded climb to the top.

Now that she was almost there, so close she could see her name on a corner office overlooking the famed Harbour Bridge and the soaring white waves of the Opera House, she felt unsettled. Nerves, she supposed. But also the acknowledgement that maybe she didn't have the killer instinct that was required in the upper echelons of big business. Miller cared too much about business practice, and sometimes that didn't play out very well.

'Now, if you'll both excuse me, I have guests waiting to play croquet on the south lawn.'

You could have heard a snail move as TJ pushed back his chair and ambled over to the door. 'By the way, Miller.' He stopped and held her unwavering gaze. 'Tell Maverick to quit stalling on taking the Real Sport sponsorship deal, would you? My people don't seem to be able to pin him down but I'm sure you can.'

And there it was. The real reason Winston International were *supposedly* being given a second chance.

Miller heard the door snick quietly closed but hadn't realised she was staring at it until Dexter muttered a four-letter word under his breath.

Miller swung her stunned gaze towards him.

'You didn't know?' He raised a condescending eyebrow.

Miller felt her face heat up, not wanting to add to her cache of lies. 'No,' she admitted reluctantly. She'd had no idea one of TJ's subsidiary companies was professionally courting Valentino. Why would she?

Dexter swore again. 'Some relationship you've got there. Does lover boy have any idea he's put a multi-million-dollar contract in jeopardy?'

'Valentino didn't do that.' Although she was silently spitting chips that he hadn't had the decency to inform her of TJ's overtures so she could have been more prepared. 'TJ did.'

'TJ's just doing business.'

'Unethically.'

'Stop being so precious, Miller. Business is business. Getting this account will boost Oracle's reputation—not to mention yours and mine.'

Miller's stomach felt as if it had a rock in it and she methodically stuffed her notes back into her satchel.

'So, do you think you'll be able to convince Ventura to do it?'

Miller strove for calm. 'I wouldn't even try.'

'Why not?'

'Because courting favours is not the way I do business.'

'TJ Lyons's is the biggest account in the country and you want it as much as I do. Maybe more. Why wouldn't you use your influence? It's not like it's any skin off Ventura's nose. In fact, I'm quite sure TJ is offering to pay him a pretty penny for the use of his pretty face.'

Miller tried not to let her distaste show. This was a side of Dexter she hadn't experienced before.

'Maybe you could give him a little more of what you gave him on the beach this morning. To sweeten the deal,' he said snidely.

Miller felt her whole body go rigid and knew she wouldn't be able to hide her reaction from him this time.

'You know, Miller,' he continued softly, 'I expected more from you than to see you romping on the beach with your lover in full view of the house.'

Ignoring Dexter, she slammed the lid of her laptop closed and fervently hoped she hadn't broken it.

She didn't have to explain herself to Dexter, but she knew if he repeated any of this back at the office it would jeopardise her promotion. It was hard enough being taken seriously at this level, despite the pains she took to always to appear confident and professional.

Dexter tapped his pen on TJ's antique desk. 'It won't last, you know. You and Tino.'

'Whether it does or not is none of your concern,' Miller

fumed, barely keeping a lid on her anger. 'And while we may have known each other at university, that does not give you the right to comment on my personal life. I'm here to do a job. That's all you need to think about.'

Dexter looked disgusted. 'Then do your job and remember that this isn't a school camp. And another thing.' He put his hand on her arm as she turned to leave. 'If we lose this campaign because of your lover, it will be *your* reputation that suffers, not mine.'

Glaring at him, Miller shook her head. 'You know, Dexter, earlier this week I could have sworn we were working on the same team. My mistake,' she finished coolly.

She heard something skitter across TJ's desk as she let herself out of the study—presumably the pen he'd been madly tapping the whole time.

'Miller! Dammit, we have to talk!'

Miller didn't stop. She had no idea what had gotten into Dexter, but she needed time and space to work out what to do next.

Tino was sitting on the bed when the door opened. Miller stood in the doorway like Medusa on a mission. He was on the phone to his sister Katrina, who was doing her best not to talk about Sunday's race and thereby placing it front and centre in both their minds.

Miller stepped into the room, her eyes sparking fire and brimstone in his direction.

Man, she was something else when she was riled— passionately alive—just like on the beach earlier. Not that he was thinking about that. He'd been honest when he'd told her it wasn't part of his plan, but watching her come apart underneath him had been possibly the most sensually arousing experience of his life, and as such it was damned hard to put out of his mind.

'Kat, sweetheart, I'll ring you back.' Glad of the excuse to end the conversation early, he dumped his mobile on the quilt cover beside him, reminding himself that he was supposed to be keeping his distance from Miller. 'Bad day at the office, Sunshine?'

She stalked across the room and dumped her computer bag and satchel on the small desk against the wall. Then she turned on him, hands on hips, her large aquamarine eyes shooting sparks.

Tino lounged back against the bank of pillows behind him. 'Are you going to tell me what's eating at you? Or is this one of those times when a woman tries to make a man's life truly miserable by making him play Twenty Questions?'

Her gaze narrowed. 'You've got that wrong. Women do not make men's lives miserable. People do that to each other.'

He stared at her and could see she was mentally wishing her words back. He wondered who had hurt her. It was obvious she didn't like talking about herself. Something they both shared, and that protective instinct she seemed to engender in him tightened his gut.

She drew in a breath as if preparing to go into battle, but her words were resigned when she spoke. 'It would have been nice if you'd told me that TJ was trying to recruit you to represent his Real Sport stores.'

'Ah.' *That* was where he knew TJ Lyons. TJ's people had been hassling his publicist to get him to become Real Sport's public representative for about six months now.

'First—' Miller's voice brought his eyes back to her '—you don't tell me that you're the legendary lothario Valentino Ventura and *nearly* make a fool of me. Now you neglect to tell me that my client wants your face and body for his online sports brand and *succeed* in making a fool of me.'

'Miller—'

'Don't Miller me.' She stalked towards him and stopped at the foot of the bed. 'You've been having fun with me right from the start of this silly charade and I've had enough. I am not here as your resident plaything and nor am I here to alleviate your boredom.'

Irritation blossomed inside him. 'I never said you were. And might I remind you that this is *your* silly charade and I'm actually trying to help you.'

'Some help when TJ all but told me the only way we would win his business is if you "quit stalling" and give him what he wants.'

Tino rubbed his jaw. 'Sneaky bastard.'

His response seemed to knock the wind from her sails because her shoulders slumped a little and her hands dropped from her hips.

'Quite.'

'I'm sorry, Miller. I didn't deliberately withhold that information from you. I get over a hundred requests of a similar nature every week and my publicist handles that side of my business. Yesterday, when I met TJ, I was aware that I knew him from somewhere but assumed it was a race meet since he was such a fan.'

She swore lightly and retreated to sit on the velour window seat, and Tino found himself fascinated by the play of light on her thick, glossy hair.

'What did you say to him?' he prompted when she remained silent.

She scowled and he noticed that her face was slightly paler than usual. 'Nothing yet. It was his parting volley.'

'A strategic tactic.'

She looked surprised that he would know such a thing, and he didn't like the fact that she still thought he had the IQ of an insect. 'You can stop looking at me as if you're surprised I can string a sentence together.'

'I don't think that.' She paused at his disbelieving look and had the grace to blush. 'Any more.'

He grinned at her honesty.

'Anyway.' She sighed. 'I'm not going to give him the satisfaction of acknowledging it.'

'Why not?'

'Because his weapon of choice is to ask his current consultants to re-pitch for the job, but if they had any good ideas they would have already given them to him.'

'They might have something new up their sleeve.'

'Nothing as good as mine.'

Tino chuckled. He enjoyed her superior confidence and kick-ass attitude. It reminded him of himself when a rookie tried to come up against him on the circuit.

He noticed her eyes were focused on his mouth, and when she raised them to his a spark of red-hot awareness flashed between them.

Clearly not wanting to acknowledge it any more than he did, she turned to face the window.

Silence filled the room so loudly he could hear the gentle ticking of the marble clock on the desk two feet away.

'Dexter saw us on the beach this morning.'

Her voice was soft, but he heard the disappointment edging her words.

Tino rolled his stiff neck on his shoulders and swore under his breath. That man was dogging his every step and he was getting beyond irritated with him.

'Are you telling me or the seagulls?' he asked pleasantly.

Miller swivelled her head around, a frown marring her alabaster forehead. 'I'm not in the mood for your ill-timed humour, Valentino.'

'What about my well-timed humour?'

She shook her head but a smile snuck across her face. 'How is it you can make me smile even when this is deadly serious?'

'Deadly?'

She sighed. 'Maybe I'm exaggerating slightly.'

Tino sat forward and regarded her silently for a moment. 'Relax. At least he no longer thinks we're faking it.'

Her smile disappeared. 'He's right about the fact that I should behave in a more professional manner with you.'

Tino snorted. 'Let me guess. He told you no touching?'

'He told me to keep my private life private—and he's right.'

'Of course he did,' Tino drawled, half admiring the man's

nous. He wanted Miller for himself, and he was trying to drive a wedge between them to get her.

Not that he could blame him. He'd realised this morning on the beach that Miller was one of those women who had no idea of her true appeal to men and, given similar circumstance, he might have done the same as Caruthers. Then again, he had yet to want a woman enough to actually fight for her.

'What does that mean?' Miller frowned.

'It means he wants you for himself.'

'No, he doesn't.'

She turned her face away, but he'd already seen her eyes cloud over.

'I can't work out if you're actually naive when it comes to men, or hiding your head in the sand.'

Her eyes flashed a warning. 'I do not hide my head in the sand.'

'Hit a nerve, have I?'

'If you're trying to be annoying you're succeeding beyond your wildest dreams,' she retorted pithily.

'If you're trying to avoid facing your colleague's attraction to you then so are you.'

She sighed heavily and turned away. 'I'm not naive. I just...' She stopped, looked uncertain. 'Can we talk about something else? Or, better still, not talk at all?'

Tino could sense the deep emotions rolling around inside her. He knew she would hate him to know the turmoil she was obviously experiencing. He didn't think he'd met a more self-contained woman, and it wasn't his experience that women kept such a tight lid on their emotions.

His Italian mother was a classic case in point—as were most of the females he'd dated, who had wanted more from him than he had ever been prepared to give. The fact that Miller so steadfastly *didn't* want anything from him made him feel ridiculously annoyed.

'This weekend really isn't going as you planned, is it, Miller?'

She had tucked her legs up under her chin as she gazed out of the window and now she glanced back at him as if surprised he was still in the room. Another blow to his over-inflated ego, he thought bemusedly.

'You think?'

Her eyes snagged on his and for a moment he was caught by how vulnerable she looked.

'You clearly dislike TJ's business methods so why do you want to work on his account so badly?'

'Partners are not made of people who say no to clients, no matter how distasteful they are.'

It took him a minute to decipher her meaning. 'Ah. You've got a promotion riding on this.'

'Something wrong with that?' Her voice was sharp and he realised she'd taken his words as an insult. He wondered what was behind her strong reaction.

'Only if you think so.'

'I deserve this. I've sweated blood for this company. I...' She released a long breath. 'It's not something you would understand.'

'Try me.'

He thought she would reject his offer, but she heaved a resigned sigh.

'It's not rocket science, Valentino. I grew up poor with a father who thought the grass was always greener on the other side and a mother who was uneducated. My mother had to work two jobs to put me through a private school so that I would have opportunities she never had. My making partner would mean everything to her.'

'What does it mean to *you*?'

He saw her throat move as she swallowed. 'The same.'

'So you dreamt of being a corporate dynamo when you were a little girl?'

He'd meant to sound light, friendly, but Miller didn't take it that way.

'We can't all have exciting careers like yours.'

Her sheer defensiveness made him realise she was hiding something from him. 'Interesting response.'

'I expect it was easy for you,' Miller prevaricated. 'Your father raced.'

'You think because my father was a racing champion my career choice was easy?'

'I don't know. Was it?'

'My father died on the track when I was fifteen. My mother still buys me medical textbooks for Christmas in the hope I'll change careers.'

She laughed, as he'd wanted her to do, but the pain of his father's death startled him with its intensity. It was as if the crash had just happened—as if a sticking plaster had just been peeled off a festering wound.

Ruthlessly shutting down his emotions he fell back on his raconteur style. 'Astronaut.'

'What?'

'Your childhood dream.'

'No.' She shook her head at his cajoling tone.

'Lap dancer?'

'Very funny.'

Some of the tension left her shoulders, but Tino still felt claustrophobic.

Jumping to his feet, he fetched a baseball cap from his travel bag. 'Let's go.'

'Where?'

'I don't know. A drive.' It was something that always calmed him.

She looked dubious. 'You go. I have work to do.'

'And all work and no play makes Miller a dull girl. Come on. It will refresh you.'

Miller sighed. 'You're like a steamroller when you want something. You know that?'

CHAPTER EIGHT

'Sorry, I only have one baseball cap,' Valentino said, holding the car door open for her.

'That's okay. My fame hasn't reached small seaside towns yet.'

He grinned at her lame joke and for some reason she felt better. Though she wasn't really interested in feeling better. What she wanted was TJ's signature on the bottom line of a contract and the weekend to be over. And not necessarily in that order.

She sighed, turning her mind away from work for once. 'Why do celebrities wear baseball caps to hide their identity?'

'Because Lyons bought all the Akubras?'

Miller burst out laughing, suddenly enjoying the fact that he was relaxed and casual. So much simpler than being uptight and serious. So much freer... Maybe there was something to recommend the casual approach sometimes.

She noticed people looking at the silver bullet as they drove down through the main part of the town. 'Bet you wish you'd brought my car now.'

He grinned. 'We'll park around a corner.'

'What if someone steals it?'

'Dante has insurance.'

'And Dante is...?'

'My elder brother.'

'What are your sisters' names?'

She sensed more than saw his pause. 'Katrina and Deanna.'

She was about to ask him another question when he pulled

the car into an empty car space and jumped out. Was that another topic of conversation that was out of bounds?

She wondered why he didn't like talking about his family and then decided to let it go. She had to remember that he wasn't with her because he wanted to be, and talking about their personal histories wasn't part of that. Nor was what had happened on the beach, but she didn't regret it. The way he had touched her had been indescribably good.

'Where are we going?' Better not to think about something she'd rather not dwell on.

'Window shopping.'

Miller raised an eyebrow. 'You like window shopping?'

'I'm looking for something.'

Narrow Victorian-era seaside shops overlaid with modern updates and sweetly dressed cafés advertising Devonshire teas lined the quaint street.

'Want to tell me what it is?'

'Nope. I'll know it when I see it.'

Despite the fact that her curiosity was well and truly piqued Miller decided to stem her need to know and show Valentino how well she could go with the flow when she chose to. Even if it killed her!

Glancing into tourist inspired shops displaying far too many knick-knacks no one could possibly want, she nearly walked into a small child when Valentino stopped outside an ice cream shop.

She looked at him and he raised a questioning eyebrow.

Ice cream? Really?

It was just what she needed and an ear-to-ear grin split her face.

She glanced at him, so big and handsome, standing in the queue, and her chest felt tight when he remembered her favourite flavour.

Deciding that there was absolutely nothing behind the gesture, but warmed by it nonetheless, she graciously accepted the cone and together they wandered into a small park.

By tacit agreement they veered towards a weathered picnic table and perched on it when Miller discovered the bench seat was covered in bird poop.

Valentino leant back on one hand, his T-shirt riding high enough to reveal the top button of his low-slung jeans, hinting at the line of hair bisecting his toned abs.

Miller swallowed and glanced around the pretty park, pretending rapt attention on the two toddlers shouting instructions at each other on the nearby play equipment. She really didn't want him to know that just the sight of him licking his ice cream and sprawled back like that was enough for her to instantly recall their tryst on the beach that morning in minute detail.

'Where did you grow up?'

His unexpected question brought her eyes reluctantly back to him, but she was glad of the innocuous topic to focus her attention away from the physical perfection of his body.

'Mostly in Queensland, but after my parents divorced my mother moved to Melbourne.'

He studied her and she forced herself not to squirm under his regard. 'How old were you when they divorced?'

'Ten.'

'And do you like Melbourne?'

'That's difficult to say. Whenever I came home from boarding school it seemed like my mother had moved to another suburb.'

'Why did she move so often?'

'We rented, and there's not much security in rentals. Which I found hard because I've always been the type of person who needs...' She struggled for a word that didn't make her seem boring compared to him.

'Certainty?'

'Yes.' Her lips lifted into a self-deprecating smile.

'Have you ever travelled?'

'No. I was always set on working and buying my own place. Even from a young age I knew what I wanted to achieve and set out to do it. That probably makes me boring in your eyes.'

Valentino shook his head. 'Determined. I know what that's like.'

Miller concentrated on finishing the delicious ice cream, feeling the tension ease out of her body. 'I guess you do.'

'So what was your childhood dream?'

Miller flashed him an exasperated look. So much for that fleeting moment of relaxation! 'I can see why you're going for your eighth world title,' she said sourly.

A wolfish grin split his face. 'I have been told I can be somewhat tenacious at times.'

'I think that's a polite way of saying you're pigheaded.'

He laughed and she liked the sound. Liked that he didn't take himself too seriously.

'Is it really that embarrassing?'

'No...' She scratched her head and then realised he had accurately read her body language and sighed, knowing his curiosity was well and truly piqued. And really it wasn't a huge secret, or anything to be ashamed of. 'When I was about eleven I dreamt of living on a huge country property. I always saw myself in a small circular room, overlooking a paddock full of horses and—'

'Why circular?'

'I don't know. Maybe because I loved *The Hobbit*...'

'Fair enough. Go on.'

'It's not very exciting,' she warned.

'Go on.'

'And in this dream I would divide my time between illustrating children's books and taking the horses out into the hills whenever I wanted.' She stopped, feeling silly giving voice to something she hadn't thought of in years. Of course she wouldn't tell him her ultimate dream. No one knew about that.

'Nice dream.'

She heard the smile in his voice and glanced at him reclining on the weather-beaten table, the afternoon sun gilding his features into a perfect mask of casual decadence.

Her heart caught and she cleared her throat, slightly embarrassed to have shared so much of herself. 'Yes, well, as my mother pointed out, it's almost every young girl's fantasy to own horses, and she wasn't paying for me to attend the best boarding school in the country to become an out-of-work artist.'

Miller heard the note of bitterness in her voice and wondered if Valentino did as well. It made her feel ashamed. Her mother had only ever wanted the best for her.

'So you stopped dreaming and took up a serious vocation?' he guessed accurately.

Regretting whatever tangent had got them onto this topic, Miller shifted and pulled her legs up to her chest. 'Dreams aren't real. That's why they're called dreams.'

'Following them gives you a purpose.'

'Putting food on the table gives you a purpose—as my mother found out to her detriment. She had me young and didn't complete her education. It made her vulnerable.'

He leant forward, his hands dangling over the front of his knees. 'And I can see why she wouldn't want that for her daughter. But I doubt she'd want you to give up on your dreams altogether. If we don't follow our dreams, what's the point of living?'

His voice was gentle and it annoyed her. Was he being condescending?

'You don't know my mum. She has a special bottle of champagne in the fridge for when I make partner.' And there was no way Miller could imagine disappointing her when she had sacrificed so much for her.

'But it's still *her* dream for you, not yours.'

She flashed him a sharp look but nevertheless felt compelled to answer. To explain herself. 'My mother has valid points.'

'I don't doubt she means well, Miller, but are her points really valid?'

His gentle query made her edgy, because it was the same one that had been taking up her head space since TJ had started subtly hitting on her.

Feeling slightly desperate, she jumped off the table and faced him. 'It would have been selfish of me to pursue art when my mother gave up so much for me.' She glanced in the direction of the sun and wondered about the time. 'We should probably get back.'

He cocked his head to the side and made no attempt to move. 'Maybe she shouldn't have pushed you so hard in the direction she saw as right. And what about your father? Didn't he help with the bills?'

She shook her head. 'I think he tried to help. For a while. But he lived on a commune, which meant that he didn't have the means to contribute to the private school my mother chose.'

'Lived?'

'He died when I was twenty.'

'I'm sorry.'

'Don't be. We weren't very close and…he died happy. Which I'm glad of now. But—' She stopped and let out a long breath. 'I don't know why I'm telling you my life story.' She *never* talked about herself like this.

'Because I asked. Why weren't you close to your dad?'

Miller snagged her hair behind her ears, memories of her father—fit and happy before the divorce—filling her mind. 'For years I was angry at him because I blamed him for my world falling apart. He just seemed to give up. He didn't once try to see me.' She swallowed past the lump in her throat. 'He later told me it was too painful.' And she suspected he hadn't been able to afford to visit her and had been too proud to lose face. 'But life is never that simple, and even though it took me a while I see now that it wasn't all his fault.'

She'd learned that one person always loved more in a relationship than the other; needed more than the other.

In this case it had been her father. Her mother's post-breakup comments had led Miller to believe that her mother had married her father mainly for a sense of security. Constantly disappointed when he could never hold down a job for very long.

Her parents had never been the greatest role models, and

Miller wasn't sure what she thought about love other than it seemed like a lot of trouble for very little return.

Her eyes sought out the toddlers, but they had gone. Instead, she watched a young couple strolling hand in hand with their large dog. But she wasn't thinking about them. She was thinking about the man beside her. Was he living his dreams? And what did *he* think about love? Did he hope to find someone special one day?

Miller felt the blood thicken in her veins at the thought. No doubt the woman he chose would be beautiful beyond comprehension and have the same relaxed attitude to life that he did. She could almost see them now—lazing on a yacht in the Mediterranean, gazing adoringly at each other, a half-naked Valentino leaning across her to seal his lips to—

Miller sucked in air and hoped her face hadn't transmitted anything of what she'd just been thinking.

'What about you?' she asked brightly, desperate to get the conversation onto any other topic but herself.

CHAPTER NINE

MILLER smiled and gazed around TJ's large living room. It held twice as many guests as it was intended to house, and absently she thought she felt as if she had just stepped into the pages of *The Great Gatsby*.

TJ's fiftieth birthday celebrations were in full swing and seemingly a roaring success: elegant women and debonair men were conversing and laughing with unbridled joy as if their lives were truly as beautiful as the party they were now attending. Some were already dancing to TJ's eighties-inspired music, while others had taken their beverages outside and were soaking up the balmy night, absently batting at the annoying insects that darted around as if they were trying to zap someone.

It was a crowd Valentino fitted right in with—especially dressed as he was now, in an ice-blue shirt that hugged his wide shoulders and showcased his amazing eyes, and tailored pants that hung perfectly from his lean hips.

'You look like you're at a funeral,' the man of the moment murmured wryly, his breath warm against her temple.

Miller sniffed in acknowledgement of his comment. She *felt* as if she was at a funeral. Ever since they'd returned from the park she had felt edgy and stressed at her sudden attack of blabbermouth. Trying to turn the tables on him had been a dismal failure. As soon as she'd asked about him he'd sprung up from the table as if an ant had crawled into his jeans.

'I'm boring,' he'd said, which loosely translated to *conversation closed.*

It had almost been a race to see who made it back to the car first. But he must have sensed her childish hurt at his rebuff because he'd glanced at her when they were in the car.

'Everything you could possibly want to know about me is on the internet.'

She'd scoffed. 'The internet tells me superficial stuff, like how many races you've won and how many hearts you've broken.'

He'd seemed to get annoyed at that. 'As I told Caruthers, if I had slept with as many women as the media proclaim I'd have hardly had enough time to enter a race let alone win one. In fact, I rarely take up with a woman during racing season, and if I do it's very short lived.'

Take up? Could he have used a more dissociative term?

'Why? Because you bore easily?'

'There is that. But, no, I usually don't allow a woman to hang around long enough to bore me. Basically women want more attention than I'm prepared to give them, so if I indulge it's usually only for a night or two.'

'That's pretty shallow.'

He'd shrugged. 'Not if the woman is after the same thing.'

'And how many are?'

'Not enough, it's true. Most want more—hence my moratorium on limiting those intimacies during the season.'

'To make sure you don't have to contend with any broken hearts that might wreck your concentration?' she'd said churlishly.

He'd smiled as if he hadn't heard her censure. 'Not much can wreck my concentration, Sunshine, but a whiny woman can certainly do damage to a man's eardrums.'

'No more than your whiny cars,' she'd shot back pithily. But then she'd grown curious. 'Don't you ever want more?'

'Racing gives me everything I need,' he'd said.

His unwavering confidence had pushed her to probe further. 'So have you ever been in love?'

'Sure.' He'd glanced over at her and Miller remembered holding her breath. 'My first love was a bright red 1975 Maserati Bora.'

'Be serious,' she'd said, and that had made his eyes become hooded, his expression blank.

'The love you're talking about isn't on my radar, Miller.'

'Ever?'

'Let's just say I'll never marry while I'm racing, and I've yet to meet a woman who excites me enough to make me give it up.' His flat tone had turned grim. 'Love is painful. When you lose someone...' He'd stopped, collected himself. 'I won't do that to another person.'

Another person or himself? Miller wondered now, sensing that part of his emotional aloofness was just a way of protecting himself from pain. His words hovered heavily in her mind, almost like a warning.

Determined the best thing she could do for herself was to forget the whole afternoon, Miller sipped at TJ's finest vintage champagne and focused on the tiny bubbles of heaven that spilled across her tongue.

'What did you say?' Valentino's low voice caused the champagne bubbles to disperse to other parts of her body and she opened her eyes to find him staring at her mouth.

'I didn't say anything.'

'You...' His gaze lifted to her eyes. 'You murmured something.'

Miller's mouth went dry and she was more determined than ever to crush the physical effect he had on her. 'Just remember that tonight I need you to be totally circumspect and professional. Discreet.'

What she was really saying was that she didn't want him to touch her, and he knew it.

'Like the other patsies you date?'

'I do not date patsies,' she said, wondering how it was that he managed to push all her buttons so easily.

'Sure you do. You date men who are learned, PC at all times, and...*controllable*.'

His assessment annoyed her all the more because she knew if she *did* date she'd look for someone just like that—except for the controllable bit. You didn't have to control *nice* men.

'While *you* hunt out blondes with big breasts and an IQ that wouldn't challenge a glowworm,' she replied sweetly.

He paused, and Miller was just congratulating herself on getting the last word in when he said, 'She doesn't have to be blonde.'

His slow smile was a signal for her to back off before she got sucked under again.

'And anything more—'

'Don't say it,' she admonished peevishly. 'I'll only be disappointed.'

His soft laugh confirmed that he knew he had the upper hand, and Miller determinedly faced the crowded room, searching for any distraction. She heard Valentino let out a long, slow breath and wondered if he was annoyed with her.

'How about we call a truce, Miller?'

'A truce?'

'Yeah. And I don't mean the kind of pact the settlers made with the aborigines before marching them off the edge of a cliff. I mean a proper one. Friends?'

Friends? He wanted to be friends and she couldn't stop thinking about sex. Great.

She took another fortifying gulp of champagne and could have been drinking his motor oil for all the pleasure it now gave her. 'Sure.'

'Good.'

God, this was awful, and he hadn't called her *Sunshine* in hours. What was *wrong* with her?

Miller was saved from the tumultuous nature of her thoughts when TJ, his barrel chest bedecked in a white tuxedo jacket, approached.

'Miller. You look lovely tonight.'

Miller's smile was tight. She didn't look lovely at all. She looked boring in her long sleeved black blouse and matching suit pants. She hadn't brought a single provocative item of clothing this weekend because she had no wish to encourage TJ's attention. And possibly because she didn't actually own anything remotely provocative. It had been a long time since she had spent money on clothing for anything other than work or exercise.

'Thank you.' She responded to the comment as she was expected to and, with civilities attended to, TJ turned to Valentino—the latest object of his fickle affections.

'Maverick. I have someone who's been dying to meet you.'

Miller tried to smile as the famous supermodel Janelle, clothed in a clinging nude-coloured chiffon creation, stepped out from behind TJ and extended her elegant hand.

A sort of mini-dramatic entrance, Miller thought sourly. Which was a little unfair, because by all accounts the model was not only considered the most beautiful woman on the planet, but the nicest as well. And she looked sweetly nervous as Valentino's large hand engulfed hers.

'Mr Ventura…'

Janelle's awed exhalation promised sexual antics in the bedroom Miller had only ever fantasised about—and with the man now staring at the supermodel no less.

'This is Janelle,' TJ continued. 'Latest sensation to hit the New York runways. But I don't have to tell *you* that. You probably have her photo up on your garage wall.' He guffawed at his own tasteless humour and then seemed to remember his audience. 'No disrespect, Miller.'

'None taken,' Miller lied smoothly. Because what she really wanted to say would jeopardise everything she had worked so hard for.

She felt Valentino tense beside her and wondered if he wasn't experiencing some sort of extreme physical reaction to the beautiful blonde. Every other man in the room seemed to be.

'Janelle.' Valentino smiled and slowly released her hand.
God, they looked perfect together. Her blonde to his dark.

Feeling like a poor cousin next to the stunning model Miller excused herself and left the men to ogle Janelle alone. No need to be a glutton for punishment.

She'd veered off from her decoy destination of the bathroom and made it to the glass bi-fold doors leading outside when Dexter appeared at her side.

'You know, Dexter, I don't know if I can go another round with you,' Miller said with bald honesty.

It was another balmy, star-filled night and she just wanted fresh air and peace.

He had the grace to look uncomfortable. 'I read some of the ideas you put down this afternoon. They're good.'

She raised an eyebrow. 'The only thing bothering me with that comment is that you seem to have expected something less.'

He tugged at the collar on his shirt. 'Can we talk?'

Resignation settled like a brick in her stomach and she extended her hand towards the deck. Might as well fulfil the fresh air component of her plan at least.

'By all means.'

Dexter walked ahead of her, but when he made to continue down the steps towards the more secluded Japanese garden Miller stayed him. 'Here's fine.'

She had no wish to recall the heady kiss she had shared with Valentino the night before any more than she already had. Not with Dexter around anyway.

Winding around various partygoers, Miller found a quiet part of the deck and turned to face him. 'What did you want to say?'

'Firstly, I wanted to apologise for being such an a-hole in the meeting earlier today. My intention was only to stop you from getting hurt.'

Miller felt a sense of unease prickle the skin along her cheek-bones. 'I've noticed that you haven't seemed yourself lately,' she ventured. 'Is something going on with Carly again?'

'No, no. That's well and truly over.' He gripped the wooden railing and seemed absorbed by the whiteness of his knuckles.

'I'm sorry to hear that.' Even though she had never met Dexter's wife, Miller hated to hear of the end of any marriage.

Dexter jerked back and flexed his hands before catching her eye. 'Come on, Miller. Surely you know what this is about?'

Miller stared at him. Shook her head. 'No.' But she did know, didn't she? Ruby and Valentino had already warned her...

'Okay, if you want me to spell it out I will.' He seemed slightly nervous. 'Us.'

'Us?' Miller knew her voice had become shrill with alarm.

He nodded, clearly warming to his subject. 'Or more specifically the chemistry between us.'

'Chemistry?'

'I want you, Miller. There's been something between us since the moment we met.'

He held his hand up and silenced her attempt to save them both any further embarrassment.

'I know you don't want to acknowledge it because we work together, but you know I've felt like this since university. My coming to work for Oracle six months ago has just made those feelings deepen. And, yes, I know what you're going to say.' He stopped her again. 'I'm your superior and office affairs don't work. But I know of plenty that have and I'm willing to risk it.'

Miller was speechless, and barely noticed when he took her hand in his. 'I've been behaving like an idiot this weekend because I haven't wanted to accept that you're really dating that pretty boy inside. Okay, I can see the appeal. But we both know it won't last, and I'm not prepared to hold my breath and wait around for it to fizzle out.'

'That's too bad, Caruthers. I would have enjoyed seeing you atrophy.'

Miller jumped at the sound of Valentino's deep, modulated voice and so did Dexter. She glanced up and was once again taken aback by the cold glint in his eyes—a stormy-grey under the soft external lights.

He looked relaxed as he regarded Dexter: *preternaturally* relaxed. In this mode she could easily see why he was going

for his eighth world championship. The shock was in the fact
that other drivers had dared go up against him in the first place.

Miller saw Dexter's chest puff out in a classic testosterone-
fuelled gesture and was horrified that he might cause a scene.
Because right now Valentino looked as if he wanted to chew
Dexter up and spit him out sideways.

'You don't have ownership rights here, Ventura.'

Ownership rights? Miller's gaze swung back to Dexter.
What was she? A car?

'Let her go,' Valentino ordered quietly, his eyes never stray-
ing from Dexter's.

Miller realised Dexter was still holding her hand and tugged
it free, wondering why it was that only French champagne and
Valentino's touch seemed to make her insides fizz with excitement.

'Miller is her own boss,' Dexter opined.

Now, *that* was more like it.

'Miller is mine.' Valentino's soft growl was full of menace.

The immediate warmth that stole through her system at his
possessive words threw Miller off-balance. How many times
had she imagined her father riding in on a white charger and
restoring her torn world to rights again? To have Valentino
stand up for her was…disconcerting. Unnerving. *Exhilarating.*

Dexter was the first to break eye contact in the stag competition going on, and Miller couldn't blame him. Even though
he was cleanly shaven, Valentino, at least in this mood, was
not a man you would cross. He was like a lethal warrior of old
who would not only win, but would take no prisoners either.

'Dance.'

Valentino held out his hand for her and she felt herself bristle
when he didn't even glance her way. Then his steely eyes cut
to hers and she forgot about being grouchy.

'Please.'

Her heart beat as fast as his silver sports car had eaten up
the bitumen on their trip down as he led her onto the parquet
dance floor.

'What's with the caveman antics?' she asked softly.

Valentino stared at her, his feet unmoving, his eyes intense, seemingly transfixed by hers. 'Playing the part of the jealous boyfriend. What else?'

Playing the part of the jealous boyfriend...

It took a moment for his words to register fully, and when they did Miller felt sick. *Playing the part. Pretending. Fake.*

The skin on her face felt as if it had been whipped, and she briefly closed her eyes against his handsome face.

If she thought she'd been embarrassed spilling all her secrets to him earlier, she now felt one hundred times worse.

Miller tried to understand why she felt so miserable. So he had stood up for her and she'd felt warmed by it? So he had been hurt by the loss of his father, as she had? So he had remembered her favourite ice cream flavour.

He was a nice person. That was all that amounted to. Nicer than she'd first thought. But at the end of the day he was still no one to her. A virtual stranger.

A virtual stranger who had brought her to orgasm within minutes of touching her. And if only she could stop thinking about *that*!

Steeling herself against emotions she couldn't immediately label, and determined he wouldn't know how she had momentarily forgotten this whole thing was fake, Miller breathed deeply and slowly.

'Just be thankful this thing isn't real between us,' he growled menacingly. 'I would have decked him if it was.'

For a horrifying second Miller wondered if he'd read her thoughts. 'For challenging you?'

'For staring at your breasts as if he could already imagine touching them. He hasn't, has he?'

Miller's eyebrows shot up. 'Of course not.'

He scowled. 'You don't want him to, do you?'

'No!'

Wow! He almost had her convinced he was seriously miffed about Dexter's interest.

'Good. And don't ever walk off on me in the middle of a conversation again.'

Miller frowned. 'If you're referring to TJ and Janelle…?' She rolled her eyes. 'I was hardly required.'

'When it comes to relationships you have no idea what's required.'

His words stung because they were true. Relationships scared her. But she was too tired to argue any more, so she shut up and let him guide her around the floor, focusing all her attention on the music and not on the way it felt to be held within the tight circle of his powerful arms. She reminded herself that she was a professional woman with goals and dreams that did not include this man in any shape or form. Reminded herself that her orgasm on the beach was a one-off and not to be repeated.

'What are you thinking?' His deep voice made her stumble and his hold tightened momentarily.

Miller's eyes met his. She was thinking that despite everything she knew about herself, about life, she still wanted to have sex with him with a bone-deep need that defied explanation.

'Miller?'

His husky command made her peek up at him from under her fringe. This wasn't her. She didn't *peek*. She looked. She organised. She…she was melting as her eyes drifted over his handsome face and her body brushed his.

Her heart beat much faster than it needed to and she wondered what type of man he really was. Why he lived the life he did. Why he had chosen to work in a profession that had taken his father's life—something she was sure affected him more deeply than he let on.

'How do you do what you do?' she asked, latching onto her curiosity about his racing life to distract herself from the fact that she seriously wanted to throw caution to the winds and have sex with him. Just once. To see what it would be like to do it with a man who just had to touch her to make her burn hotter than the sun.

* * *

Tino's hand tightened around Miller's as they continued to sway to the music. He had no idea what she was on about. His one-track mind was heavily mired in defending himself against the onslaught of her slender curves, her light, mouth-watering scent.

After their talk in the park earlier, when he'd felt a strong desire to comfort her and slay all her demons, his self-preservation instincts had kicked in and warned him that this time he really needed to keep his distance.

Of course dancing with her wasn't exactly conducive to that plan, but seeing Caruthers pawing her earlier had made him see red, and he knew he couldn't just drag her off to a secluded location feeling the way he did. Dancing with her was the safer of the two options.

'You're going to have to be a bit more specific than that,' he said, telling himself to ignore the way she seemed to fit so perfectly in his arms.

He was still a little shocked by the way he had nearly put his fist through Dexter's arrogant face. He had *forgotten* that this thing with Miller was fake. Of course that had more to do with male pride than the delicate, sensual woman in his arms right now.

Yeah, and pigs might fly. You want her and there's no shame in admitting it. Just don't do anything about it.

Just when he was about to end the exquisite torture of dancing with her, she answered his question.

'Race? Don't you ever get scared?'

Ah, she'd been asking him about his *job*.

Okay, that he could talk about on a superficial level. 'Motor racing is all about pushing yourself to the limit. There's no room for fear.'

Her body swayed against his in time to an eighties love song; the room too warm with the crush of similarly entwined bodies dancing together.

'But you push yourself *beyond* the limit, don't you? Isn't that why they call you an arrogant adrenalin junkie and a shock-jock? Maverick?'

'Don't believe everything you read about me, Miller. I'm happiest living on the edge, it's true. But I don't take stupid chances with my own life or anyone else's. Fear is an emotion. Controllable like any other. And while I'm not crazy, sometimes...' He paused, his mind automatically spinning back to the race that had taken the life of his good friend and caused him to question the sport he loved so much. 'Sometimes you have to squeeze the fear a little.'

And in this game you never look back, he silently added.

'Squeeze the fear?'

She said the words as if she were savouring a new taste on her tongue, and his body burned with a restless energy at the thought of tasting *her* again. But this time not just her mouth.

'You really love it don't you?' she said, a soft smile curving her lips.

Tino's mind jerked and went blank. Then he used his formidable mental control to switch off the erotic images turning his body hard. 'I get to experience life in its most heightened and intense form. Nothing else has ever come close.'

And probably right now he was too close to *her*—both mentally and physically. He couldn't remember ever having revealed so much about why he raced, and as for talking about his reasons for steering clear of relationships...

He frowned down at her. 'You're not going to repeat what I just said, are you?'

'You mean to a journalist?' Her tone was light, almost teasing.

'Yes.' His wasn't.

'Are your illustrious words worth very much?'

He scowled and she smiled.

'Relax.'

That captivating smile grew and he knew she was thinking of all the times he had told her to do the same thing.

'I don't need the money.'

Tino was jostled from behind by an exuberant dancer and his whole body came up flush against Miller's. Foreign emotions he couldn't name and a healthy dose of testosterone heightened as the arousal he'd been holding at bay flared instantly to life.

So much for that formidable mental control, Ventura.

He stopped dancing. 'I think it's time to call it a night.'

He noticed her face was flushed, and his arms tightened around her like a steel cage.

She stood still, looking up at him. 'I had no idea your job was so fascinating.'

His eyes became hooded and he saw his own desperate need reflected back at him from her over-bright eyes. Her lips parted softly in silent invitation and he had to fight the instinct to crush her mouth beneath his.

He studied her slender hands curled around his shoulders, her fingers elegant, the nails unvarnished. They suited her serious nature and reminded him that 'serious' females were best avoided at all costs.

'Valentino, are you okay?'

Her hands slid from his shoulders to rest lightly against his chest and he felt scalded.

Deliberately slowing his heart-rate, he evened out his breathing and stepped back from her. Every minute he spent in her presence eroded his self-control and he hated that. Without self-control he was nothing. He had no choice but to sever whatever bond had sprung up between them, because right now he sensed she was more dangerous to him than a hairpin turn at three hundred clicks.

He saw the moment comprehension dawned that he was rejecting what she was unconsciously offering and silently cursed as a moment of hurt flashed across her beautiful face.

It was as if he'd betrayed her. And maybe he had. The way he'd come on to her on the beach, then taken her for ice cream, grilled her about her life, his behaviour with her boss...

Feeling as if he owed her a massive apology, he didn't know where to start. Or if it would make the situation between them better or worse.

Then she took the decision out of his hands and closed down

her emotions as effectively as he had, pivoting on her sexy heels and walking away from him.

Immediately, an image of his father slotted into his brain, but rather than shake it off straight away, as he usually did, he let it settle there for a moment. The image was always the same. A smiling, larger-than-life hero in a white jumpsuit with a cerulean-blue helmet under his arm.

Miller's eyes.

His father's helmet.

His father's death hanging over him like a sword.

In this game, you never look back.

Tino felt his old rage at his father rear up and flattened it. This weekend was supposed to be light and easy. Relaxing. But Miller was drawing something out of him he had no wish to face, and it was messing with his head.

She was messing with his head.

He wasn't supposed to want her. At least not this much. And he sure as hell wasn't supposed to want to make her world a better place.

What a crapshoot.

CHAPTER TEN

STALKING into the breakfast room the next morning, Tino plastered what he hoped was an easy smile across his face.

Miller was there, as were TJ, Dexter and another female guest decked out in a Lycra leotard.

Tino hadn't returned to the bedroom he shared with Miller for a good two hours after she'd walked off the dance floor the night before, and when he had it had been to find her curled up in the middle of the huge bed.

He'd slept on the floor.

If you could call staring at the bedroom ceiling all night sleeping. Then he'd risen early and gone for a run, so he didn't know what mood Miller was in. By the look of the dark shadows beneath her eyes she hadn't slept much either.

'Maverick. You're up early.'

Valentino's gaze turned from Miller to TJ. He hated the familiarity with which TJ addressed him but it was one of those things that came with success. Men always thought he was their best friend and women always wanted to nail him. Well, except Miller, who might prefer to put an axe through his head after last night. He poured muesli from the selection of breakfast cereal arranged on the sideboard into a bowl and pulled out the dining chair beside the woman he was supposed to act as if he was in love with. He'd been chivalrous last night—truly, unselfishly chivalrous for the first time in his life—and he had no doubt she'd thank him for it later. Hopefully more than he was thanking himself right now.

'As are you.' He glanced at Miller and her grip tightened around the shiny fork she was using as a weapon against a grapefruit.

'Habit,' TJ said. 'No sleeping in when you're raised on a cattle station. So, are you up for a game of tennis later today?'

'Thank you.' Valentino accepted hot coffee from the maid who had just materialised at his side.

'As I explained before you insisted I have breakfast, TJ,' Miller interjected, 'I have to get back to the city by lunchtime.'

'What could be so important you have to rush back on a glorious day like today?'

Covering for her slight hesitation, Tino jumped in. 'Unfortunately I have to go over a new engine with my engineers today.'

Miller glanced up at him through the screen of her sooty lashes and he was disconcerted to find that he couldn't read her expression.

'And have you given any more thought to my proposal, Mav? To represent Real Sport?' TJ asked, confidence dripping from every word.

Not expecting such a direct question, Tino hesitated. He would have liked to tell TJ what he thought of his business tactics, but Miller stayed him with her hand on his.

'I've advised Valentino to set aside any final decisions about working on your campaign until after *our* business is concluded. I wouldn't want to muddy the waters by mixing the two—as I'm sure you can appreciate.'

The skin around TJ's eyes tightened briefly before the man recovered himself. He clearly hadn't been expecting Miller to turn the tables on him so neatly. And neither had Dexter, who started choking on his eggs.

Tino had actually been considering telling his publicist to accept the Real Sport deal in a bid to help Miller win the account, but perhaps he didn't need to. It really wouldn't affect him all that much, so long as TJ's company fitted the strict criteria he insisted on and was willing to pay one of his pet charity organisations an exorbitant sum of money for the privilege.

TJ scratched his ear in a dead giveaway of his mounting tension. 'Interesting decision. Not one I would have made.'

'Nevertheless, it's one *I've* made.'

Miller had her bushfire extinguishing voice in place and Tino felt his fists clench when he caught Dexter's murderous expression.

Easing his bulk back in his chair, his face flushed, TJ fixed narrowed eyes on Miller's boss. 'I thought *you* were supposed to be the senior consultant on this account, Caruthers?'

He didn't need to say anything else to indicate how he felt, and everyone in the room held their collective breaths.

A muscle in Dexter's jaw twitched, but Tino cut off any response he might have made with a single look. 'Miller's principles are admirable,' he said. He reached for an apple from the middle of the table. 'Qualities I would expect any company I endorse to emulate.'

For a moment no one seemed to know what to say.

'Then get that final proposal to me quick-smart, young lady,' TJ snapped. 'I want everything wrapped by race day.' He stared at Tino. 'Maybe we can even announce our collaboration at your mother's bash next Saturday night.'

Damn. If Lyons was going to his mother's party, he would expect to see Miller there.

Tino shook his head. 'I play a low-key role at that event. It's my mother's show.'

Miller stopped torturing her breakfast. 'I'll make sure I have the proposal to you in time for an early decision, TJ.' She dabbed at her lips with her napkin and stood up. 'Thank you for your hospitality and, again, happy birthday.' Then, acknowledging the other occupants in the room, she walked out like a queen.

Miller sat beside Valentino in the car as they headed back to Sydney, nursing a headache to end all others and a stomach that felt as if it was twisted up with her intestines.

She'd hardly slept the night before, completely mortified that Valentino had not only read how much she had wanted him on the dance floor, but that he had not wanted her in return. Her embarrassment from the whole trying day had been absolute.

It was a cliché that pride went before a fall, but right now Miller was grateful for the extra cushioning. In fact, she felt so terrible she almost felt sorry for the way Dexter must have felt when she had rejected him. One-way chemistry was not a pleasant thing to come face-to-face with for anyone.

'Are you okay?'

Valentino's quiet concern in the stuffy little car was the last thing she needed. 'No, not really.' She was too tired to pretend any more. 'Dexter is probably going to put me on performance management for overstepping hierarchical boundaries, TJ is livid, my promotion is most likely dead in the water, and I have the mother of all headaches.'

'If it's any consolation I thought you were magnificent this morning.'

This morning—but not last night... 'I was stupid.' This morning *and* last night.

'You'll win TJ's business and save the day. You'll be a hero.'

'Thanks for the pep talk.' She rubbed her forehead and grimaced as she thought of pulling her computer out of its bag. Still, it had to be done. She had 'squeezed the fear' and stood up to TJ this morning—which she didn't regret—but she didn't want to lose her job over it, and she knew she had major sucking up to do if she wanted to get her goals back on track.

'TJ and Dexter will expect to see you at my mother's charity event next weekend.'

Miller had heard of the Melbourne gala charity night, of course, but she'd had no idea it was Valentino's mother's event. 'I don't care.'

'If you need to attend I can arrange it.'

Miller glanced at him and winced as the sun reflected off the circular speakers on the dashboard. Was he kidding? She couldn't wait for *this* weekend to be over. The thought of seeing him again was just...horrifying. 'It'll be fine.'

He sped up and passed two cars at once. Miller tensed.

'Surely you're not still nervous about my driving?'

'This isn't a racetrack. It's a national highway.'

'With lots of room to pass. How are you going to explain your absence next weekend?'

'I'll have a headache.' Something she could easily envisage right now. Then she realised why she hadn't connected the event with him. 'Why does your mother have a different surname from yours?'

'She remarried.'

His response to the personal question was typically abrupt, and it stupidly hurt. Her brain slow to accept that her feelings were as one-sided as Dexter's.

Reaching down, she unzipped her computer satchel and opened her laptop. *Squeeze the fear?* What had she been thinking?

Tino knew the conversation was at an end the minute Miller pulled her computer out and, really, short of hurling the thing out of the window, there was nothing he could do about it. Certainly she wouldn't be pleased if he told her she looked as pale as a snowflake and should just close her eyes and rest.

And what did *he* care? He was a man who had never found it necessary to encourage female conversation, and right now, with the sound of four hundred and forty-three pound-feet of torque eating up the heated tar of the Pacific Highway he was in his element. If she wanted to work her life away that was her choice.

A little voice in his head piped up, asking if that wasn't also his choice, but he sent it packing. The difference between him and Miller was that he loved his work. He didn't want to do anything else. Whereas, while she was clearly good at her job, it wasn't her first love.

And what did love have to do with anything?

Shaking his head, he shifted his thoughts into neutral and the car into top gear and just enjoyed the peace of the open highway and Miller tapping on her keyboard.

More than once he found himself distracted by those killer legs encased in black cotton leggings when she shifted in her seat, but as soon as that happened he forced his eyes to the road and his mind to think about the important round of meetings he had lined up for tomorrow.

Thankfully she fell asleep soon after that and he reclined her seat and tried to ignore the way her soft scent filled the car. The way her hair glinted golden-brown in the sun. The way her deep, even breaths pulled her shirt tight across her breasts. He merged onto the Harbour Bridge and pulled into the left lane, jerking the steering wheel sharply right when a car he nearly cut off blared behind him.

What's your day job again, Ventura?

Thank God it wasn't standard procedure to drive around a racing track with a raging hard-on. He'd be dead at the first corner.

The sharp movement jolted Miller's head against the car door and she woke up and rubbed her scalp. 'What happened?'

'Lousy driving. Do I go left or right off the bridge?'

He skilfully navigated the rest of the way through the posh backstreets of Neutral Bay to her apartment.

The weekend was just about over and soon they'd go their separate ways. A fact that should make him feel better than it did.

'Thank you for the weekend.'

She held out her hand in a show of politeness as he pulled the car up to the kerb near the entrance to her apartment building. He could tell by the wary look in her eyes that she instantly regretted the overture, which only made him perversely take hold of her hand and hold it firmly enough that if she pulled away from him it would make her movement jerky.

She swallowed—hard—and his eyes dropped to her lips. For a second he contemplated yanking her forward into his arms and kissing her, but her mouth flattened and he knew it would be a mistake.

Clean break.

Still holding her hand, he let his eyes snag hers and felt decidedly unsettled at the glazed look in her eyes. 'I hope I fulfilled my purpose this weekend?'

Okay, now he sounded like Sam. Time to go.

'Yes, thank you.'

Again with the thank-yous.

'Good luck with the coming race.'

'Thanks.'

Valentino frowned. Another thank-you from either one of them and he was likely to ignore all his good intentions and kiss her anyway.

Climbing out of the car, he grabbed her bag and met her on the sidewalk.

'I can take that.'

She held her hand out for her bag but he only stared at it grimly. 'I know you can, but you're not.'

She hesitated, her eyes briefly clashing with his. 'Well, thank—'

'Don't.' He watched her sharply as she stepped away from him. She was holding herself a little too stiffly. Was that so he wouldn't touch her? Or...? 'You look like you're burning up.'

'I'm fine. I just have a headache.'

Tino wasn't convinced, but he wasn't going to argue with her on the sidewalk even if it was basically empty; most of the residents of this upper-class neighbourhood were safely behind closed doors.

'Let's go, then.'

He felt a stab of remorse at how exhausted she looked and knew he was partly responsible for her condition. Possibly he should have told her who he was *before* he had agreed to help her on Thursday night, but it was too late now and he wasn't a man who wasted time on regrets.

The lift up seemed to take a month of Sundays, but finally she unlocked her door and stepped inside, reluctantly letting him follow.

He glanced around the stylish cream interior of her apartment, surprised by the splashes of colour in the rugs and cushions. 'Nice.'

'Thank you.'

She remained stubbornly in the doorway and he set her rollaway case near her bedroom door. Then he looked around, perversely unwilling to say goodbye just yet.

'I said thank you.'

Tino glanced at a row of family photos on her bookcase. 'I heard you—and, believe me, you don't want to know what that makes me want to do.'

She made a small noise in the back of her throat and he knew she was scowling at him.

'Don't you have somewhere to be?'

Yeah, inside you.

He ground his teeth together as his thoughts veered down the wrong track.

Really, it was past time to go. Her prickly challenges turned him on, and the only risk he was up for right now was six hundred and forty kilos of carbon plastic and five point six kilometres of svelte bitumen.

He turned and noticed that she didn't seem quite steady in the doorway, although she did her best to hide it.

Frowning, he pulled a business card out of his wallet. 'If you need anything contact my publicist. His number is on here.'

'What would I need?'

'I don't know, Miller. Help changing a tyre? Just take the card and stop being so damned difficult.'

She held his card between her fingers as if it had teeth.

'You're not going to return the favour?' he asked silkily.

'I'm all out of cards.'

Sure she was.

'And you already know how to change a tyre.'

He smiled. He did enjoy her dry sense of humour on the rare occasions she unleashed it.

Like her passion.

Her voice sounded scratchy and he studied her face. Her

eyes had taken on a glossy sheen and small beads of sweat clung to her hairline. This time he didn't ignore the inclination to reach out and lay his palm along her forehead. She jumped and tried to pull away, but he'd felt enough. 'Hell, Miller, you *are* burning up.'

She stiffened and her eyes were bleak when she raised them to his. 'I'm fine.'

Like hell.

A moment passed.

Two.

She jerked her eyes from his and swayed. Tino cursed, grabbed her, and eased her over into one of the overstuffed armchairs facing the TV.

'It's just a headache.'

'Sit.' He headed into the alcove kitchen and flicked on the electric kettle.

'What are you doing?'

'Making you a cup of tea. You look shattered.'

She didn't argue, which showed him how drained she was. He located a cup and saucer in her overhead cupboard and a teabag in a canister on the bench and waited for the water to boil. 'What's your mother's number?'

'Why do you want it?'

She had her eyes closed and didn't look at him when she answered.

'I think she should stay over tonight.'

'She lives in Western Australia.'

'Your friend, then—what's-her-name.'

She peeled her eyes open and looked at him as if he was joking. 'No man ever forgets Ruby's name. She's in Thailand.'

There was a wistful note in her voice and he paused. 'Were you supposed to go with her?'

'I…had to work.'

He shook his head. 'Who else can I call to take care of you?'

She closed her eyes again, shutting him out. 'I can take care of myself.'

He poured her tea. 'Do you take milk?'

'Black is fine.'

As he handed her the hot tea a compelling bright yellow canvas dotted with tiny blue and purple fey creatures caught his attention on the far wall and he stepped closer. 'Who did this?'

'No one famous. Can you please go now?'

He looked at the indecipherable artist's scrawl in the corner of the canvas and took a stab in the dark. 'When did you do this?'

'I don't remember.'

Liar.

And she hadn't just wanted to illustrate children's books either; he'd bet his next race on it.

'You're very talented. Do you exhibit?'

'No. Thank you for the tea, but I don't want to keep you.'

He heard the cup rattle and turned to find her leaning her head against the back of the chair. She looked even worse than before.

Making one of those split-second decisions he was renowned for on the circuit, he grabbed her suitcase and stalked into her bedroom.

'What are you doing now?' she called after him.

'Packing you some fresh clothes.'

He upended the contents of her case on the bed and then opened her wardrobe door. He was confronted by a dark wall of clothing. He knew she liked black but this was ridiculous. He had no idea where to start.

'Do you own anything other than black?'

'It's a habit.'

So was hiding herself. 'Never mind.'

'Why are you packing my things?' Her voice was closer and he glanced over his shoulder to see her leaning in the doorway. She should be sitting down, but he'd take care of that in a minute.

'Because you're coming with me.'

'No, I'm not.'

He knew he was forcing his will on her, and it totally went against his usually laid-back style, but *dammit* he just wasn't prepared to leave her here. What if she got really sick?

Then she'll call a doctor, lamebrain. And since when have you taken care of anyone other than yourself anyway?

'It's stress and lack of sleep,' she murmured.

'I can see that. And you've hardly eaten all day either. You need a damned keeper.'

'I'm fine.'

'Consider this a long overdue holiday.'

'Don't you *dare* go near my underwear drawer!'

'It's too late. I know you like sexy lingerie.'

She groaned, and he smiled.

He threw a fistful of brightly coloured underwear into the case, pulled a selection of footwear from her closet and zipped the case closed.

He wheeled it towards her and deftly scooped her up with one arm.

'I don't like all this he-man stuff,' she said, leaning weakly against his chest.

'Too bad.' He grabbed her computer satchel and her hand-bag, slammed her apartment door behind them. 'My instincts tell me you need someone to take care of you, and I have track practice tomorrow morning I can't miss.'

Her head dropped against his shoulder. 'I have to go to work tomorrow. I could get fired.'

'Everyone's entitled to a sick day. If you're okay tomorrow night I'll fly you back. Anyway, you could get fired for *not* coming with me. Dexter wants TJ's business, and TJ wants me. You can tell Dexter you're working on me.'

He put her down to fish his car keys out of his pocket and then gently deposited her inside the car.

'I don't think that's going to impress him.'

But she rested her head against the car seat and closed her eyes.

CHAPTER ELEVEN

MILLER knew she should probably put up more resistance to his high-handedness but she felt too weak and light-headed. And some deeply held part of herself was insanely pleased by his gesture.

But she was being a sucker again. It was obvious that his behaviour had more to do with his overdeveloped sense of responsibility than it did with her as a person and she would do well to remember that.

He expertly pulled the silver bullet into the area of the airport reserved for private planes, and Miller gave up fighting the inevitable. She was so weak she had no choice but to lean into him and soak up some of his strength as he guided her towards the steps to his plane.

It was sleek and white, and she didn't feel so unwell that she couldn't be impressed. 'You're not the prime minister, are you?' she murmured faintly.

He smiled softly. 'Sorry. I'm not that big.'

Their eyes caught and held and his smile turned devilish.

'I meant that important.'

Keeping her sheltered against his broad shoulder, he led her past wide leather bucket seats with polished trim down a narrow corridor and into a room lit only by the up-lights in the carpet.

'You have a bed?' She couldn't keep the astonishment from her voice.

'I fly a lot. Hop in.'

'Don't I have to wear a seat belt for take-off?' As she said the words she felt the jet move slowly forward. Or backwards. It was hard to tell.

'Not on a private plane.'

'Does it have a bathroom?'

'Through there.' He gestured towards a narrow sliding door. 'If you're more than five minutes I'm going to assume you've collapsed and come in.'

'And you accuse me of being bossy?' She sniffed, but didn't argue. Her back ached, her stomach hurt, and her head felt as if it had some sort of torture device attached to the top.

When she came out he was on the phone speaking to someone in Italian. One of his family maybe?

God, their worlds were so different. She felt a pang as she recalled watching the cool kids all eating at the same cafeteria table at school every day while she pretended she needed to be alone to spread out her drawing pad.

'I've ordered you a light meal. It'll be delivered as soon as we're airborne.' He shoved his phone in his pocket and came towards her. 'You look like you're about to fall over, Miller. Please get in the bed.'

He might have said please but his tone implied he'd put her there in about three seconds if she didn't comply.

Slipping off her boots, she folded herself inside the cool, crisp sheets and laid her head on the softest pillow in the world...

'Come on, Miller, we're here.'

Groggy from sleep, Miller allowed Valentino to lift her out of the bed.

'Don't forget her boots,' he told someone, and Miller rested her head against his shoulder, unable to completely pull herself from the blissful depths of unconsciousness.

Seconds later she was placed in a car, and seconds after that she was being lifted again.

The next time she woke the nausea had passed and so had the headache. She stretched and felt the resistance of a top sheet.

Someone had made this bed with hospital corners. She wondered if she was in a hospital.

Opening her eyes, the first thing she noticed was that the room was in semi-darkness, with a set of heavy silk drapes pulled across the windows. The second thing was that the room was expensively furnished in rich country decor and definitely not in a hospital. She strained her ears but could only hear the faint sound of white noise. A washing machine, perhaps.

Pulling back the covers, she was pleased to see she was wearing her T-shirt and leggings from earlier. So it was still Sunday, then. She felt utterly displaced and wouldn't have been surprised if she'd slept for a week.

Feeling grimy and hot, she checked through a door and was relieved to see it was a bathroom.

Before going in she glanced around and spied her case in a corner. Flicking on the bedside lamp, she went to rummage through it for something else to put on and was surprised to discover it held only underwear and shoes.

Resting back on her heels, she let out a short, bemused laugh, remembering the exasperation in Valentino's voice when he'd asked her if she wore anything other than black.

'You're awake, then?'

Miller spun around, so startled by his voice she fell back on her bottom. Which only made him seem to fill the doorway even more. She tried not to think about how gorgeous he looked in his casual clothing. He hadn't shaved and his hair was still slightly damp from a recent shower. Then she noticed he was holding a steaming porcelain bowl.

He walked into the room and placed it on the bedside table. 'Chicken noodle soup.'

'You made chicken noodle soup?'

His lips twitched. 'My chef did.'

'You have a chef?'

'Team chef, to be precise.'

'Well...' Miller stood up, not sure what to say. 'That's very nice of you but I feel fine. Great, in fact. I did tell you I wasn't sick.'

'You *should* feel great. You've slept for nearly twenty-four hours.'

'Twenty-four hours! Are you kidding?'

'No. The doctor checked your vital signs this morning but he wasn't overly concerned. He said you might have picked up a bug and if you didn't wake properly by tonight to call him again. You spoke to him while he was here. You don't remember?'

'I have a vague recollection but…I thought I was dreaming. I know I've been pushing myself lately, but—wow. I feel fine now.'

Valentino stuck his hands into his jeans pocket. 'I'll leave you to have your soup and a shower.'

'Thanks.' Miller's mind was still reeling from the fact that she'd slept for so long. 'Oh, wait. I don't have anything to change into. You only packed…underwear and— What *is* that noise?'

He stopped at the door. 'The ocean. A cold front came through this morning so the swell is up.'

'You live on the ocean?'

'Phillip Island.'

'We're not even in Melbourne?'

'Take a shower, Miller, and join me in the kitchen. Down the hall, left and then right. There are clothes in the wardrobe. They should fit.'

Curious, Miller went to the wardrobe door and gasped when she opened it to find an array of beautifully crafted women's clothes filling the cupboard—half of them black! Wondering who they belonged to, she fingered the beautiful fabrics of the shirts and dresses, the soft wool pants and denim jeans.

But whose were they? And why did Valentino have a closet full of—she checked a few of the labels—size ten clothes?

Her size.

The thought of wearing another woman's clothing wasn't exactly comforting and her stomach tightened. T-shirts, jeans and shorts lined the shelves, and there was a grey tracksuit.

Feeling as if she was stealing the pretty girl's clothing from a school locker, Miller gingerly pulled out the tracksuit pants and a T-shirt. Thank God she had her own underwear—because there was no way she was wearing somebody else's. In fact, she'd put on her own clothes again if she hadn't slept in them for so long. The thought that she'd actually been ill was still something of a shock.

Going through to the marble bathroom, Miller quickly showered under the hot spray and opened the vanity and found the basics. Deodorant, toothpaste and a new brush, a comb and moisturiser. Brushing the tangles from her hair, Miller hunted in the cupboard for a hairdryer and came up empty.

Damn.

Without a hairdryer her hair would dry wavy and look a mess. She felt vulnerable and exposed without her things, but there was nothing she could do about it. Valentino had swooped down, got her at a weak moment, and she'd just have to brave it out. It was only clothes and hair anyway. He probably wouldn't even notice.

She walked back into the bedroom and her stomach growled as the smell of cooling soup filled her nostrils. Salivating, she perched on the bed and demolished the fantastic broth in seconds, her body feeling both clean and nourished.

But, knowing she couldn't hide out in this room any longer, she picked up the empty bowl and followed Valentino's directions to the kitchen.

His home was modern and spacious, with lots of exposed wood and a raw-cut stone fireplace that dominated a living area that was furnished with large pieces of furniture built to be used as well as to look good.

When she stepped into the modern cream and steel kitchen she was assailed with the smell of sautéed garlic and her eyes became riveted to the man facing the stove. She drank in his athletic physique in a fitted red T-shirt and worn, low-riding denims that cupped his rear end to perfection.

He was without a doubt the sexiest man she had ever seen,

and he made her forget all about being self-conscious or cautious. But she wasn't here because he was attracted to her. He'd made it perfectly clear Saturday night he didn't want her in that way, so it was time to stop thinking about the way he made her feel.

There was nothing else going on here but his over-developed sense of responsibility, and if she didn't pull herself together she'd likely make a huge fool of herself again.

Something must have alerted him to her presence because he stopped pushing the wooden spoon around the pan and turned towards her.

His eyes swept over her and she felt the thrill of his smoky, heavy-lidded gaze from across the room. She wished her senses weren't so attuned to his every look and nuance because the tension she felt in his presence made it impossible for her to relax.

Miller sensed he was holding himself utterly still, almost taut, and she was definitely using someone else's legs as she moved further into the kitchen.

'The clothes fit, then?'

She remembered the dull feeling that had washed over her when she'd first seen them. 'Yes. Whose are they?'

'Yours.'

'You bought me clothes?'

He shrugged carelessly at her stunned tone and added tinned tomatoes to the pan. 'Technically Mickey bought them.'

'Mickey?'

'My Man Friday.'

He had a Man Friday? One who knew his way around women's fashion? She hated to think how many other women Mickey had clothed at Valentino's request.

'Mickey runs interference between all the people vying for my attention and makes sure my life runs smoothly. Calling up a department store and organising a few items of clothing for a woman was a first.'

'I didn't say anything.' She felt impossibly peeved that he'd read her so well.

'You didn't have to. You're very easy to read.'

'Not usually,' she muttered.

His slow smile at her revelation made breathing a conscious exercise.

'Why didn't you just pack me something other than underwear and shoes?' Realising she was still holding the empty soup bowl she set it down on the benchtop between them. 'That would have made more sense.'

'Probably,' he said. 'But I saw all that black in your wardrobe and panicked. And I have a soft spot for your lingerie and shoes. How was the soup?'

'Divine.' Miller felt flustered by his admission about her underwear. 'I'm not keeping the clothes,' she said stubbornly. 'There's enough there for ten women.'

He leaned against the lacquered cabinet beside the stove. 'Mickey's ex-army—a complete amateur when it comes to what women need.'

'Whereas you're an expert?'

His eyes studied her in such a way that goosebumps rose up on her arms. 'So I've been told.'

Miller sighed deeply, searching around in her mind for some way to change the subject and lower the tension in the room to a manageable level. It would be too embarrassing if he guessed how disturbed she was in his presence.

'I should probably get going. I've taken up enough of your time.'

'I'm cooking dinner.'

'I thought you had a chef?' She tried to make her tone light but she wasn't sure she'd pulled it off.

'He provides the food. I cook it when I'm here.'

'What is it?'

'Not poison.'

He gave a short laugh, and she realised she'd screwed up her face.

'Relax. If you want to go home after dinner I'll arrange it.'

Just like that, she thought asininely. Did nothing faze this man?

Yes. Talking about his family. His father. The accident that had claimed the life of his friend. He had his demons, she knew, he just kept them close to his chest.

Miller nodded. She felt stiff and awkward, and when she wetted her painfully dry lips his eyes locked onto her mouth with the precision of a laser. She felt the start of a delicious burn deep inside.

So much about this man stimulated her to the point that she could think of little else. Which made staying for a meal a questionable decision. Wasn't it playing with fire to spend any more time in his company?

A vague memory of him feeling her head and administering a drink of water to her some time during the day filtered into her mind. His gentleness and consideration of her needs was breaking down all of her defences against him. Something she really didn't want. Lord only knew what would happen if he showed any indication that he wanted her half as much as she wanted him. She wasn't sure she would say no. Wasn't sure she *could* say no.

Spotting his phone on the far bench, her mind drifted to work.

'Did you happen to bring my phone yesterday?' she asked, wondering if she still had a job and if it was too late to call Dexter. She'd done nothing on TJ's account all day, so chances were slim, but she'd rather know than not.

He stopped stirring the sauce on the stove. 'It wasn't in your handbag?'

'No.'

'You can borrow mine. But if you're calling work don't bother. They know you're with me.'

'Sorry?' She forced her eyes away from the muscled slopes of his arms. 'What did you tell them?'

'That you were sick.'

Miller barely suppressed a groan. 'Why did you do that?'

'I presumed you'd want your workplace to know where you were and you weren't capable of telling them.'

Miller knew he was right, but it didn't change the fact that she was irritated. 'I have to finish TJ's proposal, and I'm still not sure Dexter isn't planning to put me under a formal performance review. Now he'll just think I'm skiving in order to spend time with you and definitely do it.'

'After his own behaviour over the weekend he'd be crazy to question yours. I'm sure your job is perfectly safe. And everyone's entitled to a sick day. I bet you have almost a year's worth accumulated by now.'

Miller blushed. He made her feel like a goody-two-shoes. But his championing of her gave her a warm glow that was hard to shake.

Something she could never rely on long term, she reminded herself. Especially with a man like him.

'You have a point.' Hopefully one Dexter recognised. 'But still, I can take care of myself.' She tried to hide her irritation but it wasn't easy. Everything about her response to him—and his lack of one to her—was just debilitating.

He flicked a knob on the stove and put a lid on the saucepan, his gaze never shifting from hers as he prowled towards her. He rounded the island bench and Miller felt her breathing become choppy. She knew it wasn't just because of her rush of irritation.

He stopped just shy of touching her, his blue-grey eyes piercing, his arms folded across his chest. *'Thank you, Tino, for helping me out Sunday night when I felt like something the cat had dragged in,'* he said mockingly.

Miller felt ashamed of her stroppy behaviour. What was *wrong* with her? 'Thank you, Tino, for helping me out Sunday night when I felt like something the cat had dragged in.' And probably looked it…

'That's better.'

His smile could have melted a glacier. Then his eyes locked onto her hair and she suddenly remembered that it wasn't straight, as usual, and probably looked terrible.

She raised a self-conscious hand. 'Wavy.'

He reached out and looped a semi-dry curl around a finger. 'Pretty.'

She shook her head and his finger snagged on the curl, pulling it tight. She shivered. 'I prefer it straight.'

His hand drifted to the side of her face, his fingers following the curve of her jaw. 'That's because it gives you a sense of control. I like it either way.'

Miller's breath stalled in her lungs at the way he was looking at her. She could read desire in his eyes. Want. Intent, even. She was shocked by it because previously she had assumed his interest in her wasn't real. But now she suspected he had just been resisting the chemistry between them on Saturday night—as she had done for most of the weekend. As she should still be doing...

Only she felt powerless to look away from the banked heat in his gaze and a thrill of remembered pleasure raced through her body. A thousand reasons as to why this wasn't a good idea pinged into her mind, but overwhelming her logical thinking was a wicked, sinful sensation that refused to go away.

All her life she'd done the right thing. The proper thing. Working hard to get good grades and make her mother proud, building a reputation at work that would ensure her future was secure, shelving the more risqué side of her nature. Until now that had been enough. Satisfying, even.

But Valentino brought out a delicious craving in her that was impossible to ignore.

CHAPTER TWELVE

TINO saw the sharp rise and fall of Miller's chest as his finger lingered on the side of her jaw, felt her tremble as he deepened the caress. He hadn't intended to touch her, seduce her, but now he could think of nothing else.

Some part of him hesitated. Really, if he had any integrity he'd stop. She'd been sick. She was a guest in his house. But none of that registered with her standing in front of him looking gorgeous and tousled, her cheeks pink, her lips softly parted. God, he wanted to kiss her. He wanted—

She swayed slightly towards him, pressed the side of her face into his palm. 'Valentino...?'

Her blue eyes were huge, shining with an age-old invitation that sent every ounce of blood in his body due south. Breathing felt like an effort, and it would have taken more strength than he possessed not to lean in and kiss her.

So he did.

Lightly. Gently. Just their mouths and his hand on her face connecting them.

And maybe he would have stopped so that they could eat the dinner he'd prepared, but after the slightest of hesitations she rose onto her toes, flattened herself against his chest and he was lost.

His hands moved to span her waist and curled beneath the fabric of her T-shirt to sweep up and down the smooth skin of her back. She whimpered. He groaned, angled his head, took the kiss deeper, his mouth hardening as the hunger inside him threatened to consume them both.

Her hands found his hair; his found her breasts. Those perfect round breasts.

'Miller...' Her name was a deep rasp and she wrenched her mouth from under his as his thumbs flicked across both nipples at once. She arched into his hands, her back curving like an archer's bow, and he growled his appreciation, pushing her bra cups down to pluck at her velveteen flesh more firmly.

Her sensitivity and responsiveness completely undid him, and he lifted her and turned to place her on the stone bench.

'Valentino.'

Her desire-laden sigh stalled him. He pulled in a tanker full of air and tried to steady himself as his eyes met hers. He flicked his tongue over his lips and saw her pupils dilate as she watched him.

Forking a hand through her thick waves, he forced her eyes up to his. 'Miller, I want to be inside you more than I've wanted anything in my life. Tell me you want the same,' he ordered gruffly.

He felt the thrill of desire race through her and her lips parted, her fingernails digging into his shoulders. 'Yes. I feel... I want the same thing.'

Tino's eyes grew heavy with fierce male triumph and his hands confidently moved to the waistband of the sweats she wore. 'Lift up.'

He dragged the pants down her legs, admiring her red lace panties before they dropped to the floor. 'God, I love your lingerie.' He spread her thighs wide and pulled her forward until her bottom was balanced on the edge of the bench. 'Take off the T-shirt and bra.'

She complied, and he leaned forward to capture one pointed nipple into his mouth. He suckled her. Bit down lightly. His hands steadied her hips as she jerked under the lash of his tongue. She was perfect.

'Beautiful,' he breathed. He switched his attention to her

other breast, loving the feel of her fingers speared into his hair, holding his head hard, her small whimpers of arousal testing his self-control.

He felt her hips push against his restraining hold and knew she was seeking pressure at her core. Pressure he couldn't wait to give her. He moved one hand between her legs and urged her thighs wider, opening her, his eyes momentarily closing as he revelled in the feel of his hand sliding through her curls and over her delicate folds. She was already wet and his middle finger slipped easily inside her. She made a sound like a sob, her hands clutching at him as he stroked her sweet spot with his thumb.

His erection jerked in an agony of wanting.

Soon, he promised himself. He curved his other hand around the nape of her neck and pulled her eager mouth back to his, adding another finger into her body and setting up a steady rhythm.

She groaned, a deep, keening sound, and ground herself against his hand. He felt the urgent lift of her body that signalled she was close to coming, but as much as he wanted to feel her orgasm gripping his fingers he wanted something else more.

'Lean back on your elbows.'

He waited while she shifted the empty soup bowl out of her way and then he bent forward and nuzzled her, his tongue stroking and teasing the bundle of nerve endings at the top of her sex.

She bucked against him so hard she nearly dislodged him, and he wound his arms around her waist.

'Damn, Miller, you taste so good.'

His husky words sent her over the edge and she came like a shot around his tongue. He nearly disgraced himself in his own kitchen.

Calling on every ounce of focus, he rode her orgasm with her. Then he stood, rose above her, pulled his T-shirt up over his head and shucked his jeans around his ankles. Her head was still thrown back on her shoulders, her breasts pushed high, her body open for his viewing pleasure. His eyes drank in the sheer beauty of her for all of two seconds and then he shifted closer, positioning himself between her splayed thighs before—

Condom.

Right. *Hell.*

He reached around and pulled one out of his back pocket, sheathed himself.

'Are you always this prepared?'

Her husky words and wary gaze stayed him. His usual approach would be to make a sarcastic quip. Keep things light. But her scent was warm on his tongue and for some reason he couldn't conjure up anything light.

'No. But after touching you on the beach Saturday I've dreamt of nothing else since.'

'Nothing else?'

Her tone was teasing and it gave him permission to tease her back. 'Maybe my mother's lasagna.'

She smiled, her eyes slumberous as she took him in. His erection throbbed under her perusal and her startled eyes flew to his.

His hands tightened on her hips. 'Do you want me to stop?' The words felt as if they were ripped out of his throat with a pair of pliers, but he needed to be sure she was totally on board with this.

Her eyes held his. 'Would you?'

'Of course.' Though it might kill him.

'No, I don't want you to stop.' She leaned forward, gripped him in her palm. She closed her eyes as her fingers explored him. 'I want to feel you inside me.'

He wanted that too—so badly his legs were shaking with need. He pulled her hands from his body before he lost it. 'Open your eyes.' His voice was a husky command and it seemed for ever before she raised her sleepy gaze to his. 'I want to see your eyes as I fill you.'

Her eyes widened and her tongue touched her lips as she nodded.

'Hold on to me.' She draped her arms along the line of his

shoulders and gripped the back of his neck. Tino pulled her firm breasts against his torso and lifted her.

He'd intended to take her hard, his instinct to plough himself into her, but some sense of civility whispered that this first time he might hurt her, so instead he lowered her with as much care as he could.

Even so, he felt the hiss of air against his temple as her body encircled him.

She was tight. So tight. He stilled. 'Are you okay?' Sweat beaded his forehead as he forced himself not to jam her on top of him.

She wriggled her hips and adjusted herself around his girth and his head nearly came off.

'Now I am.' Her voice was so damned sexy. Like her smell. 'You're just…big.'

Women had told him that before, but never had those words sounded so sweet.

'You can take me,' he growled, kissing her brow.

'I think I already have.' There was laughter in her voice and then he shifted his hips and surged forward, giving her more.

'Or not.' She groaned. 'I want more.'

God, so did he.

'Hook your legs around my waist.' He could barely speak. The urge to pound into her was overwhelming but he needed a soft surface for what he was about to give her—otherwise she'd end up black and blue.

Somehow he made it to his bed, but when he fell on top of her he was so close to coming he didn't hold back. Her body clung to his as if it had been made just to please him, and when he felt another orgasm building inside her he didn't know how he managed to hold off long enough to take them both over the edge together, but he was so damned glad he had.

God, had sex ever been this good?

Miller lay still, unable to move, and yet stricken with the urge to run for her life. She had just had wild, unrestrained sex with one of the beautiful people. Someone so far removed from her real world she couldn't even leap to see the platform he lived on.

And it had been amazing. He'd filled her so completely, so powerfully, all she'd been able to do was cling to him as he'd carried her into his room and then carried them both into a miracle of erotic pleasure.

At least it had been for her. For him it was probably run of the mill. *She* was probably run of the mill. Trying not to let her old insecurities swamp her, Miller clung to what was real. Which, ironically, was that this was fake.

Her sickness, his bringing her here—none of that had changed anything between them. And would it matter if it had? She had her goals, her plans for the future, and she wasn't looking for a relationship. She wasn't looking to fall in love with anyone yet.

She understood the fundamental rule that one person always loved more than the other, and she also knew that relationships were unstable at best and downright destructive at worst.

And it wasn't as if Valentino was going to insist on having a relationship with her! He'd probably prefer to be hit by one of his fast cars. And even if he did his job took him all over the world. She knew herself well enough to know she'd never cope with the uncertainty of having a relationship with someone who left her all the time. *Would* leave her as soon as he was bored.

But that still wasn't the scariest thought churning through her right now. No, the scariest thought had been the sense of connection she had felt when Valentino had joined their bodies together. It had been as if a missing part of herself had slotted into place. A ridiculous notion, and one that made her think that the sooner she got her life back to normal the better.

Valentino shifted beside her and Miller tuned into the laboured sounds of his breathing, the only noise in the otherwise silent room.

'You're thinking again.' His low voice rumbled from deep inside his chest.

'It's what I do best.'

'I think we've just discovered another occupation you could channel your energies into.'

Miller smiled weakly, and then gasped as he rolled on top of her and lightly pinned her to the bed. He fisted a hand in her hair and tilted her face up to his. She swallowed. He was so primal, so male. His hold was both possessive and dominant, and it shouldn't have thrilled her as much as it did.

'What are you thinking about?' he persisted.

'Isn't that my line?'

'I think it's pretty clear what I'm thinking about. What I want to know is if you're regretting what just happened between us.'

No, she wasn't regretting it. She was trying to figure it out. 'No. I probably should, but I don't.'

'I'm glad.'

He laid his palm across her forehead and Miller swallowed past the lump in her throat. 'I'm fine. I told you that.'

'I'm allowed to check.' Leaning down, he ran his tongue over her lips, stroking into her mouth as she automatically opened for him.

Miller gasped as pleasure arrowed straight to her pelvis, turning her liquid. She moaned when his knees urged hers wider and he settled himself between her thighs.

'I want you again,' he murmured roughly.

'Really?' Miller felt him hard between her legs and her trepidation at being here with him evaporated as she sensed just how wrong she had been about this chemistry being one-sided. He wanted her. Badly. And the knowledge gave her a giddy sense of sensual power that amazed her.

CHAPTER THIRTEEN

Tino woke up early, as usual, and smelt the scent of sex at the same time as he registered that Miller was no longer in his bed.

Confounded, he cracked an eye open and was even more puzzled to find the room empty and silent except for a couple of magpies warbling outside his window.

He was used to a woman clinging after a night of sex. Not that he remembered ever having a night quite like that. He'd been insatiable, and a grin split his face as he recalled how she had matched him the whole way.

He stretched his hands above his head and flexed stiff muscles. Last night had been incredible—and against every one of his rules.

Sort of.

It wasn't that he'd forbidden himself to have sex this close to race day, it was getting involved emotionally that was the no-go zone. He might have thought about Miller more than he would have liked over the past couple of days, but he knew now that he'd had her in his bed his interest would start to wane. It always did.

Which was why it was good that she would be leaving this morning. He had an enormously busy week, made even more so because he'd had to cancel yesterday's round of meetings to care for Miller.

Rolling out of bed, he pulled his jeans on and went in search of her to find out what time she wanted him to get the jet ready.

He found her outside, watching the sun rising over the ocean that stretched beyond his backyard. She was completely enveloped in his black robe—so appropriate, he mused—her hair mussed and wavy, the sun's rays highlighting the gold in amongst the brown.

She turned when she heard the sliding door open and fingered her hair self-consciously. She looked adorable. And uncomfortable.

He immediately sought to put her at ease and ignored the whisper of apprehension that floated across his mind. He didn't doubt for a minute his ability to control this situation between them.

'What are you thinking?'

'I didn't know men wanted to know what women were thinking so much.'

He studied her, feeling as if he was facing down one of Dante's highly strung thoroughbreds. 'I don't want to know what women are thinking, I want to know what *you're* thinking.'

'I'm thinking that you have a beautiful home. For some reason I took you as a city type.'

'I visit too many cities as part of my job. My mother lives on the other side of the island and I bought this place when she fell ill a couple of years ago.'

'Is she okay now?'

'Fine. Fitter than I am.'

Miller's lips twisted into a faint smile. 'Well, it's lovely here. Peaceful.' She glanced out over the lawn towards the beach and he caught the nervousness in her eyes. 'But I should probably be heading back home.'

Her lips were still kiss swollen from last night, and he noticed a slight red mark from where his beard growth had grazed her neck. He'd have to be more careful of her soft skin, though some primal part of him was pleased to see his mark on her.

'It's seven in the morning. Are you sore?'

She coloured prettily. 'That's personal.'

'Sunshine, it doesn't get any more personal than my mouth between your legs.'

She gasped. 'You can't *say* that!'

She looked mortified, and for some reason her reaction pleased him. He was so used to women preening and posing in front of him that her embarrassment was refreshing. She hadn't been a virgin, he knew that, but she wasn't a practised sophisticate either, and one of the things he loved—hell, *liked*—about her was that she was so easy to tease.

He stepped closer to her and urged her stiff body into the circle of his arms. 'I've embarrassed you?'

'Yes, but I don't know how.' She gave a deep sigh. 'I should have expected you to just say what you think. It's one of the first things I noticed about you.'

She gripped his forearms as if to hold him off, but he'd have none of it, his thumbs drawing lazy circles over the thin cotton of his robe covering her lower back, gentling her until she fitted against him as naturally as his tailor-made jumpsuit.

'What else did you notice?'

'That you had ripped jeans and needed a shave.'

Tino gave a hoot of laughter. 'Sunshine, you are hell on my ego.'

'Your ego is one area I would never worry about.'

She was watching his mouth, and his laughter dried up instantly. 'I usually start the day with a run followed by a green smoothie, but this morning I'm going to make an exception.'

Her aquamarine eyes lifted to his, her pupils expanding as he watched. 'What are you replacing it with?'

He enclosed the nape of her neck with his hand, slowly bringing her mouth to his. 'That depends on the answer to my earlier question.'

She frowned, and he pressed his pelvis into her to facilitate her memory recall. She smiled, and he felt tightness in his chest.

'Only a little.'

Her answer sent the tightness lower. 'I promise to be gentle.'

Miller must have dozed, because she awoke to the feel of Valentino spooning her from behind as he had done first thing that morning. Then she had slipped out of his bed, because the sensation of waking with his protective arm draped around her waist, his fingers resting protectively over her abdomen, had been both frightening and exhilarating. And now the same feelings were back.

He just seemed to swamp her. His warmth, his scent, her desire to burrow against him and never leave. It was as instinctive to her as breathing.

Right from the beginning she'd sensed he would have this intense effect on her, and wasn't that the reason behind her fear now? Hadn't she avoided feeling such intense emotions for another person because she knew better than most how tenuous relationships were? But how could a playboy racing car driver with a reputation for having a death wish make her feel so…so safe? So secure? It had to be straight hormones because otherwise it defied logic!

As did her current feeling of wellbeing. Something she hadn't experienced since before her parents had divorced, she suddenly realised. And hot on the heels of *that* little revelation was the unwelcome understanding that she had been trying to get this same sense of belonging from her job for years.

On some level that wasn't a total surprise, because she had always treated work as a second home, but what *was* newsworthy was that even the thought of making partner didn't give her quite the same sense of safety that Valentino did right now.

Confused, and feeling slightly exasperated with her see-sawing emotions, Miller again tried to creep out from under his arm—only this time his strong fingers spread out like tentacles to cover her whole belly.

'Am I going to have to tie you to my bed to make sure you're still here when I wake up?'

His deep voice was sleep-rough, his warm breath stirring her hair.

Miller stilled, wanting to run and wanting to stay at the same time. In the end she wasn't strong enough to resist his magnetic pull and subsided back against his hard body.

'Where were you going, anyway?'

'I really need to start making tracks.'

'Now, *there's* a very Aussie expression.' He rolled her onto her back and rose up on one elbow, his gunmetal-grey eyes lazily intense between thick, dark lashes.

Feeling exposed, Miller pulled the sheet up over her breasts. His gaze lingered on the sheet and she had the vague impression that he was about to flick it off her.

Glad when he didn't, she let her breath out slowly.

'Why are you so determined to run off, anyway? You don't strike me as the one-night-stand type.'

'I'm not.'

'Then stay one more day. I have a sponsors gig tonight. You can come with me.'

Alarmed by just how much she wanted to accept what she suspected was an unplanned invitation, Miller immediately reacted in the negative. 'I can't. I have to work.'

Annoyance flickered briefly across his face. 'Work from here. You have your computer.'

Miller smoothed her eyebrows. He was doing his steamroller thing again, but what was one more day to him? And when would she go home? Later tonight or in the morning?'

He stroked a strand of hair back off her forehead. God, she must look a mess.

'I know what you're thinking. You don't like the uncertainty of it.'

Miller's eyes flashed to his. Did he really know her that well, or was she really that easy to read?

'It's not hard to figure out, Miller. I know you hate surprises so it follows that you wouldn't like half-baked plans. How about we make it the whole week?'

The whole week!

'Five days, to be exact. That way you can come to my mother's gala event, which TJ is expecting to see you at anyway, and watch me race on Sunday.'

Miller felt her brows scrunch together. 'Why would you want me to come to your mother's ball?'

Tino rolled onto his back and gave her a reprieve from his intense scrutiny. 'Honestly? My mother invites every debutante in the known universe to this thing and expects me and my brothers to meet every one of them in the hope that we'll fall in love.'

His apathetic attitude to falling in love stabbed at something inside her. 'Oh, poor you. All those single women in one room. I would have thought it was every man's dream.'

Her words were sharper than she had intended, but she was slightly insulted that he would talk about other women while he was in bed with her. Even if they were women he apparently didn't want.

The reminder that he would never want anyone permanently—not even her—struck a chord, because permanence was all she did seek! She'd just never sought it with a man before.

'Hardly.' His dramatic tone nearly made her laugh, despite her aggravation. 'Debutantes come with strings attached, stars in their eyes and pushy mothers. That's no dream any man I know has ever had.'

Suddenly, he lifted onto his elbow, looming over her again, and Miller caught her breath. His gaze roved over her face and he trailed a finger over the sensitive skin of her neck just below her ear, winding a slow, sensual path downwards.

'I did you a favour last weekend. The least you can do is protect me from women I'm not interested in on Saturday night.'

His voice had lowered with intent, and Miller's body responded like one of Pavlov's dogs. She pushed his hand away. 'Stop that. I can't think when you're this close.'

'That's only fair since you have the same effect on me.'

'I do?' For some reason, his admission startled her.

'Well, I *can* think, but it's usually about one thing.' His hand returned and his fingers circled her nipple, making her arch off the bed. 'Say you'll stay.'

She tried to organise her thoughts. 'Because of the sex?'

She was breathless, and his smile as he rolled on top of her was one of pure male triumph. 'The sex is phenomenal, but the more I think about you going to my mother's party the more I like it. With you there I can relax, and I might even enjoy it. And Caruthers will expect it.'

'Since when do you care what Dexter thinks?' Miller asked breathlessly, catching a moan between her clamped lips as his fingers traced a figure eight over first one breast and then the other, skimming over her nipple just a little bit too lightly each time.

'I don't.' His skilful touch became firmer. 'Say yes.'

Miller felt deliciously light-headed. 'You're steamrollering me again,' she accused, trying to hold her body still.

Valentino nipped the skin around her clavicle. 'Is that a good thing?'

Giving up on trying to resist him, she speared her fingers through his hair, enjoying the thick, weighty texture of it curling through her fingers.

'I don't know.' She groaned and dragged his mouth to her breast. 'Please, just stop talking.'

'You're so sexy.' His voice was rough, more a low growl, as he *finally* pulled her nipple into his mouth with just the right amount of pressure.

Miller felt as if she was levitating as her legs shifted helplessly under the onslaught of pleasure. She moaned his name. He nudged her legs apart, and even though her internal muscles ached from over-use the rush of liquid heat between her thighs was instant. She felt him fumbling in his side table, his mouth briefly leaving her breast to tear the condom packet open, and then he was back, pressing her into the bed.

'Now, where was I?'

God, he made her feel… He made her feel…

'Say you'll stay.'

His mouth teased the soft skin beneath her ear, and even though she knew she must have terrible morning breath she turned her face, searching for his kiss.

'Okay.'

What had she just agreed to?

'For five days.'

His fingers stroked between her legs, drawing moisture from her body in preparation for his possession.

'I…' She arched her hips, her body already balanced on a knife-edge of pleasure, desperate to go over.

'Say yes.'

'Yes—whatever.'

She was desperate, and his husky chuckle of dominance annoyed her. With a spurt of defiance at his formidable self-control in the face of her total lack of any, she wrapped her legs around his hips and tilted her pelvis so that he had no choice but to slide deep.

He swore as he plunged into her, and Miller smiled and buried her face against his straining neck. She clenched his shoulders and her internal muscles at the same time, and suddenly the balance of power shifted as he bucked in her arms before surging deep again.

She felt him groan against her hair, and then her mind closed down as he pounded into her with such primal force she thought she might break. And then she did. Into a whirlpool of pleasure that sucked her under and blew her mind. Dimly, she heard Valentino shout her name, and she could feel the power of his release as he spilled himself inside her.

It seemed for ever before either one of them moved, and even then it was only weakly.

'Are you okay?' he asked.

Miller gulped in air. 'Ask me in a minute.'

He chuckled and shifted onto his stomach beside her. 'Sorry. That was a bit rough.'

Miller stretched her arms above her head. 'It was fabulous. I may never move again.'

Groaning, Valentino dragged himself from the bed. 'I wish I had the same luxury. Unfortunately not working yesterday and spending half the morning in bed today has no doubt put the team incredibly behind.' He bent and gently kissed her lips. 'Why don't you stay in bed? Recover? I'll send Mickey with a car at five o'clock to bring you into the city.'

The city? It took a minute for Miller to remember their conversation. She watched through half-closed lids as Valentino strolled into the bathroom and turned on the shower.

She recognised that she'd just been steamrollered *again*, and that she had agreed to stay with him for five days and attend a party to help keep eager debutantes at bay.

What were you thinking?

She stared at the ceiling and tried to feel agitated, but instead all she felt was happy. Oh, not at the whole debutantes thing, but just at being here. Maybe it was called afterglow.

Otherwise it didn't make sense. Especially given her confused emotions and the fact that she still didn't know if she had a job or not. But, yes, she was definitely happy.

But she was also smart enough to know that she couldn't rely on those feelings. Reality would intrude and she would have to get herself back on track. In the meantime maybe she should take his suggestion. Call Dexter, finish TJ's proposal, and then treat the next five days as an impromptu holiday.

Valentino, she knew, would make sure she had fun—and would it be so wrong to soak up his hospitality for a little longer? To soak *him* up for a little longer?

She rolled onto her stomach and glanced at the digital bedside clock. Ten o'clock. If this was a normal work day she'd have been hard at it for three hours by now and staring down the barrel of another ten. And those were her hours during quieter periods.

She sighed and shifted her attention to the magpies hopping about and conversing with each other outside the full-length window that took up one whole wall of Valentino's masculine room.

She was under no illusions as to why he had asked her to stay for five days, and although she had never been the type to enter into a purely sexual relationship there was a first time for everything. She just had to keep things as light and breezy as he did. No intense emotions, no second-guessing herself at every turn. Just…fun.

Miller stepped from the car and smiled at Mickey as he held the door for her. Mickey was everything she'd expected—large, fit, and capable of lifting a small house with his bare hands. The fact that he was also capable of purchasing women's clothing didn't bear thinking about.

The pavement outside the swanky Collins Street retail outlet was lined with photographers and fans, all of whom quickly lowered their cameras as soon as they saw that she wasn't anybody special. Glad for once not to be part of the in crowd, Miller quickly turned her eyes to the burly security guards who stood either side of the short red carpet.

Swallowing hard, she was just contemplating how foolish she would feel if she gave them her name and they rejected her when a woman in a chic black suit rushed forward.

'Ms Jacobs?'

'Yes.'

Thank God. Someone knew her name.

'My name is Chrissie. Mr Ventura asked me to show you in.'

Miller smiled, ready to kiss Valentino's feet for his thoughtfulness. Straightening her spine, she followed Chrissie into the brightly lit store.

Faces turned towards her but she ignored everyone as the attractive aide wound a path between glamorous, laughing guests holding sparkling glasses of wine and champagne. The room was buzzing with energy and it grew steadily more frenetic the further she went—until Chrissie stepped aside and Miller knew why.

Valentino stood in the centre of a small circle of admirers wearing a severely cut pinstriped suit and an open-necked snowy white shirt. He looked so polished and poised, so sinfully good-looking, her mind shut down and all she could do was stare.

Having chosen black trousers and a gold designer top carefully from Mickey's inspired collection, and redone her hair in
its normally sleek style, Miller still felt utterly exposed, stripped
bare, when Valentino's eyes honed in on her like a radio device
searching out a homing beacon.

God, she was in trouble. Big trouble. He was just so beautiful, with his dishevelled sable hair and five o'clock shadow, and
her body knew his, had kissed every inch of him. The urge to
bolt was overwhelming, but then he smiled and she exhaled a
bucketload of air. It would be all right. She was fine.

Her toes curled in her strappy heels as he walked towards
her, his eyes glittering.

'You look beautiful,' he murmured as he captured her hand
and brought it to his lips in an age-old gesture.

Miller's stomach flipped and she couldn't tear her eyes from
his. 'Funny, I was just thinking the same about you. Though
I wasn't going to mention it on account of your ego and your
current cheer squad, lapping you up like Christmas pudding.'

Valentino threw his head back and laughed and Miller felt
riveted to the spot. Did he have any idea that he was so completely irresistible? Yes, of course he did. The people around
them couldn't take their eyes off him.

'How did you spend your day?' he asked, smiling down at
her.

'I worked—'

'Now, *there's* a newsflash,' he teased.

'Yes, well. I spoke to Dexter, and although he hasn't forgiven
me for what I said to TJ I don't think he's going to do anything
to jeopardise my promotion.'

'Good.' He grabbed a glass of champagne from a passing
waiter and handed it to her. 'When are you going to start paint-
ing again?'

Miller was exasperated that he had discovered her most secret dream.

'Valentino, don't ask me that.'

'Why not?'

'Because it was a childish dream.'

'Not childish. Daring. A dream unhampered by adult limitations. Perhaps it's time you stopped hiding behind that wall you protect yourself with and go fot it.'

'I will if you will.'

The instant the words were out she held her breath, her heart hammering.

His eyes pierced her but there was no hostility behind them, just reluctant admiration. 'I forgot you were such a shrewd operator. Come on—I have to mingle.'

That easily he closed her down, and although it made her feel slightly hollow inside she refused to address the feeling.

With Valentino beside her she felt carefree, as if he had flicked a switch inside her, and as much as she fought against the uncertainty of her emotions she felt more like herself now than she ever had.

She watched him handle a group of business executives with ease and aplomb and for a moment envied him his sheer confidence and charisma. There was just something about him that was devastatingly attractive—and it wasn't just the way he looked. It was his sense of humour, his chivalry, his deep voice, his keen intelligence...

Miller sucked in a breath as a shot of pure terror made her chest hurt.

She was falling for him.

No. It couldn't be true. She wouldn't let it be true. But...

As if sensing her distress, Valentino turned to her, his eyes intense as they swept over her. Burned into her.

'Miller, are you okay?'

Miller stared up into his concerned gaze.

'I'm fine,' she answered automatically.

His gaze narrowed, sharpened, and Miller had a horrible feeling that he could see into her deepest self.

His hand reached for hers. 'You're sure?'

No, she was far from sure. But what could she say? That she

thought her feelings for him were deeper than his for her? She shook her head, and his frown deepened.

Realising she was behaving like a nutcase, Miller pulled herself together. She *wasn't* falling in love with him; she was too smart to do that.

CHAPTER FOURTEEN

HE really should be worried about getting himself into the mental space required to win pole position for tomorrow's race but for some reason he wasn't. The race was less than twenty-four hours away, and he wondered if he had time to make a quick detour on his way to the track.

He probably should be worried about how he felt about Miller as well, but so far he'd refused to think about it—and he was going to continue doing so until after the race.

It was true he was starting to entertain some thoughts about not finishing things with her straight away...but the jury was still out on that one.

And it wasn't just because of the sexual pleasure she brought him—though that was astounding. It was that he liked being with her. He'd even let her convince him to try Mexican food yesterday. He smiled at the memory. He hadn't planned on eating much—his team manager would have thrown a fit if he'd deviated from his strict diet this close to a race—but he hadn't needed discipline to tell her he'd pass.

'What are you thinking about?'

He glanced at her, sitting beside him in his Range Rover, her long legs curled to the side. The question had become a running joke between them since Monday night.

'That bean mixture you tried to force-feed me yesterday.'

'Enchiladas.'

He shuddered, and she rolled her eyes.

'I did not try to force-feed you. There must be something wrong with your tastebuds.'

'I promise you there's nothing wrong with my tastebuds, Sunshine.' He watched her blush and brought her fingertips to his lips.

He grinned as she smiled, and the sudden realisation that he was relaxed and happy jolted him. Often he had to force those feelings, but right now they were as genuine as she was.

'Any news from TJ?' He knew the man had agreed to part of Miller's business proposal, but the crafty old bastard was holding back on the rest until he found out his own decision about representing Real Sport.

Miller had insisted that he not do it, but he'd turned the matter over to his publicist anyway.

'Not yet. But I'm confident he'll give us the rest of his business in due course.'

Tino was too, but talking business reminded him again of one of his own little projects that he'd neglected of late.

Deciding that he had enough time, he turned the car off the next exit ramp, just before the Westgate Bridge, that led to the backstreets of Yarraville.

'This isn't the way to Albert Park,' Miller said, curiosity lighting her voice.

'I want to show you something first.'

He pulled into a large empty car park and cut the engine.

'This is a go-carting track.'

'Yep. Go Wild.'

Miller followed him out of the car, her sexy legs encased in denim jeans and cute black boots.

'Why are we here?'

'I want to check it out.'

'I think it's closed.'

'It is.' He reached the double glass doors and used a key to open it. 'I bought the place two months ago, when I was bored convalescing. I've had a lot of work done on it, but I haven't been back for a while.'

He walked into a dimly lit cavernous room, the smell of grease, sawdust and petrol making him breathe deep. A sense of wellbeing settled over him as he took in the changes since the last time he had visited.

Miller walked past him, clearly impressed by the view of a twisting track that took up most of the space.

She wrinkled her nose. 'It smells of stale chips.'

He hadn't noticed that.

'I think the kitchen is the next thing to be overhauled. This is the little kids' area,' he explained, walking towards one of the barriers. 'The bigger kids' track is out back.'

'Do we have time to see it?'

'Sure—hey, Andy?'

'Tino. I wasn't expecting you.' A tall, lanky man in a plaid shirt that had seen better days and grease-streaked jeans loped towards them.

Tino clasped his friend's hand. 'Andy, this is Miller Jacobs. Miller, this is my centre manager and fellow visionary, Andy Walker.'

'Hello.'

Miller took Andy's hand and Tino was slightly annoyed with himself for automatically stepping into her personal space when he registered Andy's very male appraisal of her.

They might be sleeping together right now, but that didn't mean she belonged to him in any way. The words he'd thrown at Caruthers at the weekend—"Miller is *mine*!"—reregistered in his mind and pulled him up short.

'Tino?'

He blanked his expression and cast off the unsettling notion that he'd well and truly crossed into a no-go zone with Miller. 'Sorry, I missed that last bit.'

'I said the main track is finished,' Andy repeated. 'Did you get my text last Wednesday?'

'I did. That's why I thought I'd stop by.'

'Come on. I'll show you.'

Clamping down on his worrying thoughts, Tino followed

Andy towards the rear of the building and out into the bright sunshine, shielding his eyes as he took in the track.

'It's huge.' Miller exclaimed behind him. 'Like a mini-racetrack.'

Tino smiled. 'That's because it is.'

'I know that,' she scoffed. 'I just wasn't expecting it to be that big.'

'Want to go out on it?'

'You mean walk around it?'

'Not walking.' He turned to Andy. 'Any chance you can pull a couple of carts out?'

'Sure.'

Andy grinned like a happy Labrador and Tino enjoyed the look of surprise on Miller's stunning face.

'I've never driven a go-cart before.'

'There's nothing to it.'

Five minutes later they were both kitted out in helmets and gloves, and once he'd fixed Miller into her cart he climbed into his own.

'We're not racing each other,' she informed him nervously.

Wondering if she would get the bug, he smiled. 'Remember it's just like driving a normal car only the gears are on the steering wheel and there's no clutch. Right foot is accelerator and left is brake. Other than that there's nothing to it.'

He watched as she revved the engine, unexpectedly distracted when her face glowed. 'One more thing,' he called above the throaty whine of the carts. 'These engines are more powerful than the usual carts, so go easy on the first few laps. I'll go first, so you can follow my line as you learn the track.'

'Ha—you're going first because you can't stand being second.'

Valentino smiled. She'd got that right.

He gunned his engine and put the cart into gear. The carts were fixed with a side mirror, so he kept his eye on her as they did a couple of laps.

Both he and Andy had designed the carts, and he was impressed at how well they handled.

After five laps he pulled his cart to a stop near the starting line and waited for Miller to pull up beside him.

'How was it?'

Her face was flushed from the light wind and her eyes were glowing with excitement. Oh, yeah, she definitely had the bug.

'I think you could turn me into a speed demon.' She grinned. 'This is *amazing*. But they seem a bit powerful for kids.'

Valentino found himself once again captivated by her smile, those eyes that shifted from aquamarine to almost indigo when she was aroused. 'They're for big kids. Teenagers, adults. This is a specialised track.'

'Great to hire out to corporations for bonding sessions.'

'Maybe.' He hadn't thought that far ahead yet.

'I have an idea.'

She leaned towards him conspiratorially and his eyes instantly fell to the deep V the movement made in her black T-shirt.

'What?'

'I'll race you!'

It took him a second to get his mind off her cleavage, and by that time she was already two cart lengths ahead of him. Valentino felt his competitor's spirit champing at the bit.

Little witch. She had deliberately distracted him.

As he followed her the feeling that he was very much in trouble with this new, more relaxed Miller returned. In fact, possibly he'd been in trouble all along.

He'd sensed this latent fire in her nature many times over the weekend at TJ Lyons's, and after listening to her story about her childhood he could see how she had locked herself down to a certain extent to achieve her goals. Which he admired. It took a lot of fortitude to achieve what she had done, and even though he felt that her reasoning had been a little skewed by her mother's fears, he couldn't fault her execution. She'd de-

vised a plan for herself and she'd worked diligently to achieve
it. A bit like himself.

Tino kept pace with her, challenging her lead on one of the
easier corners but never taking over. For once he was happy to
take the back seat in a competition.

He came up beside her and signalled one more lap. He saw
determination set in her face and had to smile. If she but knew
it he could take her in a heartbeat.

He upped the pressure as they headed towards the home
straight and his heart nearly exploded in his chest as her cart
veered to the side and headed full speed towards a railing that
had yet to be lined with safety material.

'The brake! Dammit, Miller, hit the brake!'

He knew she couldn't hear him, and he was powerless to do
anything but watch. It was like seeing his father head towards
that concrete barrier all over again. The feelings of pain and
loss were so powerful, so ferocious, he tasted bile in his mouth.

By some dumb stroke of luck her car pulled up an inch before the railing. Tino vaulted out of his cart and wrenched her
helmet off before he'd taken his next breath.

'What were you *thinking*?' he all but bellowed as he took in
her wild eyes and laughing face.

'Oh, my God. I nearly hit the rail!' Her voice was vibrating
with both adrenalin and mild shock.

'That was a bloody stupid thing to do.'

'I didn't mean to,' she said indignantly. 'My heel got caught
under the brake pedal.'

Her heel… Tino glanced down at her feet and noted the delicate heels on boots he'd only seen as cute. Damn, he hadn't
even considered her footwear when he'd made the impromptu
decision to take her out on the track.

He swore under his breath. Ironically, he'd never felt more
scared of anything in his life than seeing Miller hurtle towards
that railing.

'Hey, relax.' She was still smiling as she pulled herself out
of the cart. 'It was just a bit of— Oh!' She threw her hand out

and gripped his forearm as her legs buckled beneath her weight. 'My legs feel like jelly.' She laughed and locked her knees. 'I think that was better than sex.'

Tino shook his head, his sense of humour gone. 'Those carts top out at sixty ks an hour. You could have been seriously hurt.'

And why was he yelling at her when it was his own fault?

'I'm sorry if you were worried.' She tightened her grip, suddenly becoming aware of his over-reaction at the same time as he did.

'Of course I was worried. I don't think we have insurance on this place yet.'

'I don't know what to say.' She looked stricken. 'Are you okay?'

Tino collected the helmets. 'Fine.' He clamped down on his emotions with vicious intent, doing his best to stanch the fierce male rage that flooded him. The desire to grab her, crush her up against the nearest wall and pump himself inside her was like a savage animal riding him hard.

Instead, he shook his head, trying to clear his thoughts, and stalked off towards the equipment room. He could see Andy striding across the track and deliberately headed in the other direction. He needed to do something. *Hit* something.

'Tino!' Miller called after him, and he could hear her clipped footsteps on the concrete behind him. He lengthened his strides. 'Tino?'

Dimly he registered that she had stopped walking, and he pivoted around and stared at her. Her beautiful face was pale with concern. She approached him with the caution of a lion tamer without a whip and chair.

'Don't walk away. Please.'

Her quiet voice set off a riot of emotions, and right up there with wanting to physically take her—to physically *brand* her— was the urge to hold her and keep her safe. For ever. And that was the moment he realised he was shaking.

With the kind of lethal precision that was used to construct one of his beloved racing cars Tino shut down everything inside him.

'I have to get to the track. I've wasted enough time here.'

CHAPTER FIFTEEN

'MA's finally got her wish, I see.'

Valentino turned at the sound of his older brother's voice and kept his irritation in check. He'd been enjoying a moment's quiet after being inundated with well-wishers and pseudo-virgins at his mother's charity extravaganza all night, but fortunately now the guests seemed to have settled—chatting, dancing and enjoying the view from one of Dante's premier hotels.

'What's that?' he asked, feigning interest.

'One of her sons has found love at her famous event.' Dante glanced towards the dance floor where Miller was dancing.

Tino glowered at him. 'I'm not even going to pretend I don't know what you're getting at.'

'That's good. We can cut straight to what you're intending to do about it instead. Should I be shining my shoes?'

'Not unless you're planning to go back to school,' Tino said lightly. 'I'm not in love with Miller,' he added dismissively. 'In case that was your next inopportune comment.'

He'd rather Dante harangue him about the big race tomorrow than a woman who was already constantly on his mind. He glanced at the dance floor where Miller was teaching his twelve-year-old nephew to waltz, and his body throbbed at the pleasurable memory of their lovemaking an hour earlier when he had returned to their penthouse suite.

Not that he'd meant it to be lovemaking. What he'd meant it to be was rough and raw sex to put them squarely back on the footing they'd started out on.

He'd spent six stressful hours at the track, secured second off the grid for tomorrow's race, and endured a gruelling press conference that had focused as much on his new "girlfriend" as it had on tomorrow's race.

All day he'd ignored his over-reaction to Miller's near accident, and the effort it had taken to keep his emotions under lock and key and be able to perform on the track had worn thin.

When he'd returned to the room and found Miller standing beside the bed in a demi-cup bra and matching thong he hadn't even bothered to say hello.

He frowned, memory turning him hard as a rock.

No, he hadn't said hello. She'd glanced up, half startled to see him as he'd prowled silently into the bedroom, and then she'd been against the wall and he'd been between her legs before he'd even thought about it.

He'd barely leashed his violent need for her, and yet once again she'd been right there with him. And, just as she had a tendency to do, she'd managed to twist the final few minutes of their coupling so that he was no longer the one in control. This time she'd insisted that he look at her with just the whisper of his name, and they'd flown over the edge together in an endless rush of pleasure.

Her sweet mouth still looked a little bruised, and as for the dress she had on... He took back his declaration that Mickey knew nothing about women's fashion. The chocolate-brown silk and froth creation clung to every curve and set off her eyes and skin to perfection. He'd never actually seen a more beautiful woman in his life, and his latent fear of tomorrow's race paled in comparison to the feelings she raised in him.

She was in his head—hell, she had been in the car with him at the track that afternoon, and that couldn't happen.

'You haven't taken your eyes off her all night and you've barely gone near her,' Dante drawled.

Tino tipped the contents of his glass of iced water down his parched throat. 'That's your definition of love?' he mocked, forcing his tone to reflect bored nonchalance. 'No wonder you struggle to keep a woman.'

Dante laughed softly. 'That's my definition of a man who's still running.'

'Let me repeat,' Tino bit out. 'I am not in love with Miller Jacobs.'

'What's the problem with it?' Dante was watching Miller now, his eyes alight with admiration. 'It was bound to happen some day. You're a lover, Tino, not a fighter. And she *is* stunning.'

'You're calling me soft?' He ignored the instinct to go for his brother's throat.

'I'm telling you I think she's great, and if you don't go get her I might.'

Valentino knew Dante was baiting him but even so his brother's soft taunt twisted the knots in his gut.

'Okay.' Dante held up his hands in mock surrender, even though Tino hadn't moved a muscle. 'I take back the not a fighter bit... But seriously, man, why fight it?'

Tino turned his back on the dance floor. 'You know why.' He sighed. 'My job.'

'So quit.'

Tino was shocked by Dante's suggestion. 'Would you give up your multi-billion dollar hotel business for a woman?'

Dante shrugged. 'I can't imagine it, but...never say never. Isn't that the adage? You've done it for fifteen years and you have an omen flapping over your head the size of an albatross. I don't think your time will be up tomorrow, if that helps, but why risk it?'

Tino knew Dante was remembering the day his father had crashed, something neither brother ever talked about, but he felt better now, knowing the reason behind Dante's topic of conversation. 'Did Ma or Katrina put you up to this?'

'You think the girls tried to get me to stop you racing? Ma would never do that. She's always been a free spirit. No.' He shook his head. 'There was just something different about you on the track today. As if you were...'

He frowned, searching for a word Tino didn't want him to find.

'Distracted.' *Yep, that was the one.* 'I thought maybe you were thinking it was time for a change.'

'In conversation, yes,' Tino bit out tersely.

The fact that his brother had noticed his earlier tension before the qualifying session was more concerning to him than if either one of the females in their family *had* sicced Dante onto him.

'Fair enough.' Dante took the heavy silence between them for what it was—disconnection. 'I won't push it. God knows I'd hate someone to push me. But I'd avoid Katrina if I were you. She's already trying to work out who will be flower girls to Toby and Dylan's pageboys.'

Miller stood to the side of the sparkling room, only half listening to Katrina's friendly chatter, her body still tingling from Valentino's earlier lovemaking when he had returned from the track. He hadn't even greeted her when he'd walked into the room—just backed her against the wall like a man possessed and taken her.

It had been fast and furious, and although he had shown her the same consideration as always she couldn't shake the feeling that he had been treating her as just another pit lane popsy— someone to use and discard straight after.

After her near accident at the go-cart track that morning his emotional withdrawal had been handled with military-like precision.

Which on some level she understood. She had been a complete bag of nerves watching him whip his car around the track during the qualifying sessions at speeds that made the go-carts look like wind-up toys, so she could only imagine how badly he had felt when she had lost control of the cart.

What she couldn't understand—what she *hated*—was the

way he politely maintained that everything was still normal between them.

It was too much like the time her parents had sat her down to tell her they were separating, pretending that they were happy with the decision while they each seethed with anger and hurt below the surface.

Their denial of how they really felt had made dealing with the separation nearly impossible, because Miller had *known* something wasn't right, and yet the one time she had been brave enough to broach the subject with her mother she had brushed her off and made her feel stupid.

Which was why, she realised, she had let Valentino give her the silent treatment. She hadn't been brave enough to open herself up to that kind of hurt again.

Unfortunately, that wasn't a failsafe plan, because without her even being aware of it the unthinkable had happened.

She had fallen in love with him.

The uncomfortable realisation had hit her when she'd been pressed deliciously against the hotel wall with his body buried deep inside hers.

At that moment when he had looked at her a spiral of emotion had caused her heart to expand, and she'd shattered around him in an agony of pleasure and longing.

She'd told herself it wasn't possible to fall in love in such a short space of time, but her heart had firmly overridden her head—as it had always done with Valentino Ventura.

And now, feeling like a liferaft set adrift, she understood why people did crazy things for love. She understood what her father had been talking about when he'd said that it was too painful to visit her after she had left with her mother. He'd had his heart broken. The sudden wave of understanding made her eyes water.

Blinking back the memories, she smiled at Katrina and pretended she'd been listening—and then at her next words she really was.

'I never thought I'd see my brother so in love. He can't stop looking at you.'

Couldn't stop looking at her? He hadn't looked at her once.

Well, okay, she had seen him glancing her way a couple of times, but she'd have called that glowering at her, not the benign version of *looking*. And he'd turned away each time before their eyes could properly connect.

Which was ironic, because she was supposedly here to prevent him from being accosted by every unattached woman at the ball, and since they weren't behaving like a couple the women had been lining up to get to him in droves. In fact, if she'd known he was going to completely ignore her, she would have brought a numbering system to help the whole process go more smoothly. Sort of like a speed dating service. Give everyone their five minutes and wait for him to choose her replacement.

Miller felt a spurt of anger take over from the intense pain that thought engendered, and latched onto it.

He might not want to continue things with her, but that didn't give him the right to treat her so poorly. It wasn't as if she would suddenly develop into a needy person who wouldn't let him go. She had known it was going to end. What she hadn't expected was that she would enjoy being part of a couple so much. She had been so fiercely independent for so long the thought hadn't occurred to her. But with Valentino… He made her feel so much. Made her want so much. Was that why he was avoiding her so thoroughly? Had he guessed her guilty secret?

The thought that he had horrified her. She might feel as if she was ready to face a lot of things she hadn't before in her professional life, but personally she was very far from ready to "squeeze the fear". Certainly not with a man who would never feel for her the same way she felt for him.

But it was one thing to deceive her workplace about her relationship with Valentino, which she had hated doing, and quite another to deceive Valentino's loving family. She didn't think Valentino would care if she corrected Katrina.

'Actually, Valentino isn't in love with me.'

'Oh, I wouldn't be so sure. He might not have said—'

Miller put her hand on Katrina's arm. 'I only met Valentino last week. The only reason I'm here with him now is because he helped me out of a bind and pretended to be my boyfriend.' She saw Katrina's eyes widen with unbridled curiosity and shook her head. 'Don't ask—it's a long story. Suffice it to say I became unwell, Valentino helped me out, and…here I am. But I'm going home tomorrow.'

Katrina turned compelling blue-grey eyes on her. 'But you have feelings for my brother?'

Miller inclined her head. No point in denying what was clearly obvious to Valentino's sister. She shrugged. 'Like every other woman on the planet.'

'So you're going to do what he does?' Katrina gently chided.

Miller's brow scrunched in confusion.

'You're going to make light of it?'

'No, you're wrong. I don't make light of anything.' She gave a self-deprecating laugh. 'I'm way too serious; it's one of my faults.'

Katrina pulled a face. 'I know my brother can be intensely brooding and unapproachable at times, but don't give up on him. He's protected himself from getting hurt for so long I think its second nature to him now. After our father's death he changed, and not—'

'Giving away family secrets again, Katrina?'

A biting voice savagely cut through his sister's passionate diatribe and Miller cringed. He stood behind her, legs braced wide and larger than life in a superbly cut tuxedo that made him look even more like a devil-may-care bad-boy than his jeans and T-shirts.

'Hello, little brother. Are you having a good time?' Katrina greeted him merrily.

'No. And I need to go. I'll see you at the track tomorrow, no doubt. Miller?'

He held out his arm for her to take and Miller did so, but

only because she didn't want to cause a scene in front of his sister. 'It was lovely to meet you, Katrina.'

'Likewise.' Katrina leant in close. 'Don't let his scowl put you off. He's harmless underneath.'

Oh, she was so wrong about that, Miller thought miserably. Valentino had the power to hurt her like no one else ever had, and she was really peeved she had given him that power over her. Because it was her own stupid fault. He'd been honest right from the start.

Halfway across the room, Miller tugged on his arm. 'I might stay on a bit longer, if that's okay?'

God, when had she been reduced to sounding like a Nervous Nelly?

'Why?'

Because I don't want to go upstairs with you in this mood and have you rip my heart to pieces.

'I'm having a good time.'

'I don't want you talking to my family about me *or* my father.'

His voice was cold and she now wondered if he really was leaving because he needed to get sleep and prepare for the race tomorrow, or because he assumed she'd keep trying to wheedle secrets out of his family about him.

'I didn't ask Katrina anything,' she denied. 'She assumed that you had feelings for me. We both know you don't and I told her this whole thing was fake.'

Valentino grabbed her elbow and pulled her to the side of the room to let a couple pass by.

'Why would you say that?'

Miller forced herself not to be intimidated by his frown. 'Because I don't like being dishonest and I like your family.'

'This thing stopped being fake the minute we had sex and you know it,' he growled.

Miller's hopeful heart skipped a beat. Did he mean that? Could his black mood be because he had strong feelings for her and just didn't know how to express them?

'What is it, then?' She knew she was holding her breath but she couldn't help it.

He raked back his hair in frustration and glowered at the glittering crowd of doyennes behind her. 'I don't know. Good fun?'

Good fun?

Stupid, desperate heart.

'Look, I'm sorry. I've had a terrible day and I don't want you talking about my father. The man died racing a car. Everyone needs to get over it and move on.'

'Like you have?'

His scowl at her quietly voiced question didn't bear thinking about. 'Don't psychoanalyse me, Miller. You don't know me.'

'Only because you hide your deepest feelings under solid cement.'

She thought he would try and make light of her comment. When he didn't she realised how stressed he really was. She also realised that her breathing had grown harsh, and the last thing she wanted to do was argue with him the night before a crucial race.

'Valentino, your sister didn't mean any harm. She was boosting me up because she thinks that you protect yourself against being hurt.' A conclusion she had also drawn after talking to him that day in the park.

'That's ridiculous.'

'Is it?' Miller asked softly, her heart going out to this wounded, gorgeous man. 'Or is it that you believe that your father didn't love you enough to quit racing? Because I know that tomorrow's race has been playing on your mind, and I've seen enough to guess that maybe you're a little angry with him.'

A flash of insight hit her as she recalled how stiff he had been in his mother's company—a woman she knew he loved dearly.

'Maybe even with your mother—although I'm not sure why that would be.'

'Don't confuse your mother issues with mine, Miller,' he snarled.

Miller gasped. 'That's a horrible thing to say. My mother

did her best and while you've helped me see that I've blindly followed her dreams instead of my own that wasn't her fault. It was mine. I didn't *have* to give up my artistic aspirations. I *chose* to because it suited me at the time.' Miller felt as if he'd torn a strip off her and left her bleeding. 'Now, I can see I've overstayed my welcome, so if you'll ex—'

'Don't leave.'

Miller's stomach was in knots and she was shaking. She *had* to leave before her runaway mouth said anything more she might regret. 'I'm tired.'

'I don't mean right now. I mean tomorrow. Quit your job and travel with me. Come to Monaco next week.'

Miller stared at him. The tinkling chatter of happy guests faded to a low hum. He didn't look completely comfortable, but was he serious?

'Why?' she blurted out.

'Why does there have to be a reason? Haven't you had fun the last few days?'

Miller smoothed her brows. 'You know I have. But it's not enough to sustain a relationship.'

'Why put a label on what's between us?'

Miller paused, taking in the offhandedness of his question, his effortless arrogance.

Oh, God, he wasn't talking about having a relationship with her. Not a real one, anyway. *She* was the only one here with long-term on the brain.

'I...can't.'

She knew if she took him up on his offer it would mean a lot more to her than it did to him, and she knew herself well enough to know that it would be hell on her self-esteem. It would also be repeating the same mistakes she had made in the past— because following him around the world would be following *his* dreams at the expense of her own.

Reluctantly, she shook her head.

'Why not?' He sounded frustrated. 'You hate your job.'

'I don't hate my job.'

He made a patronising noise and swung his arm in an arc. 'It's not what you want to do.'

'How would you know? You never ask me what it is I want— you just tell me.' She knew that was slightly unfair but she wasn't about to correct herself right now. This was about protecting herself from his clear intent to change her mind for his own selfish purposes.

'If you don't want to come just say so, Miller, but don't use your job as an excuse.'

'What has got into you?' she fumed. 'You've been like a bear with a sore head all day, you've ignored me all night, and now you're trying to steamroller me again to get what you want.'

'Because I *always* get what I want.'

Miller rolled her eyes. 'That's arrogant, even for you.'

He shoved a hand in his pocket, pulling the divinely cut tuxedo jacket wide in a casually elegant move redolent of a 1950s film. 'You didn't seem to mind it this week.'

Didn't seem to... Miller couldn't fathom his indifference. She had feelings and he was treating her as if she was here just to please him.

'I don't know how serious your offer to travel with you was, but I'm assuming you want a relationship. I have to tell you that I would never enter into something with a man who is so stubborn and selfish and *angry*.'

'And finally she lists my faults.'

'Oh, that is *so* typical of you—to make fun of something so serious.'

'And it's so typical of you to make serious that which could be fun.'

Miller drew in a fortifying breath. 'I think we've said enough. We're too different, Valentino. You want everything to be light and easy, but sometimes feelings aren't like that.'

'I know that. It's why I refuse to have them.'

'You can't just refuse to have them. They're not controllable.' But Miller had the uncomfortable realisation that she had once believed exactly that.

Valentino rocked back on his heels. 'Every emotion is controllable.'

'Well, you're lucky if that's true, because I've just discovered that mine aren't, and I can't be with someone who only connects with me during sex because he's too afraid to share how he feels.'

'It's the damned uncertainty of it you don't like.'

Miller threw up her hands. 'And now you're going to tell me how I feel in an effort to hide your own feelings.'

'Fine—you want to know how I feel? I feel that my father made a bad choice when he married my mother. He wasn't a man equipped for having a family and he was never around for us. Hell, I was his favourite because of our shared love of adrenalin highs, but even then we hardly had any time together. And when his car hit that wall—' He stopped suddenly, his voice thick. 'I won't do that to another person.'

The words *it hurts too much* hovered between them and Miller's stomach pitched.

'Valentino, I'm so sorry.' She wanted to touch him, but his stiff countenance stole her confidence.

'You're not coming with me, are you?'

Miller swallowed heavily. If he had shown any inclination that his feelings might be even close to being as strong as hers she'd stay. She'd...

No. She couldn't stay for anything less than love. She refused to fall victim to the laws of relationships. She refused to be in an unequal partnership and watch it wither and die. Because it would take her along with it.

'I can't. I—' She hesitated, fear of being ridiculed stopping her from exposing exactly how she felt, but knowing she loved him too much just to walk away without trying. 'I want more than you're prepared to give.'

He raked back his hair in frustration. 'How much more?'

'I want love. I never thought I did, and I'm still afraid of it, but you've made me see that working so hard, cutting myself off from my true passions, from my *feelings*, is living half a life. I'm sure I won't be any good at a real relationship, but I'm ready to try.'

He turned his head to the side, his expression hard. 'I can't give you that. I don't do permanence.'

Miller smiled weakly, her heart breaking. 'I know. That's why I didn't ask it of you. But thank you for last weekend. For this week. And good luck tomorrow.'

'Fine.' His voice was harsh, grating. He cleared his throat. 'Tell Mickey when you want to organise the jet.'

Miller felt her lower lip wobble and turned away before the tears in her eyes spilled over. It didn't get much more definitive than that.

CHAPTER SIXTEEN

WHEN Miller disappeared from view Tino stalked off without a clear destination in mind, burning with anger. Didn't she know what a concession he had made for her? What he had just offered her?

Tino stopped when he found himself outside on a tiered balcony, staring sightlessly at the glittering city lights.

Thank God she *hadn't* taken him up on his offer. What had he been thinking? He *never* took a woman on tour.

'I'm probably not the best person to follow you out here, but I know at least out of respect you won't walk off on me.'

Valentino turned to find his mother standing behind him.

'Want to talk about it?'

No, he didn't want to talk about it.

'Thanks, but I'm fine, Ma.'

'Don't ask me how this works.' His mother stepped closer. 'But a mother always knows when one of her children is lying. Even when they're fully grown.'

Valentino blew out a breath and tipped his head to the starry sky. He really didn't want his mother bothering him right now, and he cursed himself for not leaving when he'd had the chance.

'Ma—'

His mother held her hand up in an imperious way that reminded him of Miller. 'Don't brush me off, darling. I once let your father go into a race in turmoil, and I won't let my son do the same if I can help it.'

Valentino stared down at the tiny woman who had the

strength and fortitude of an ox, and his anger morphed into something else. Something that felt a little like despair.

She stood beside him and the silence stretched taut until he couldn't stand it any more. 'You found it hard to be married to Dad with his job. I know you did.'

'Yes.'

'Why didn't you ask him to quit?' Valentino heard the pain in his voice and did his best to mask it. 'He would have done it for you.'

She regarded him steadily. 'You're still angry with him. With me, perhaps?'

He turned back to the lights below; cars like toys were moving in a steady stream along the throughways. Miller had said he was angry and right now he *felt* angry, so what was the point in denying it?

'I never realised just how much you closed yourself off from us after your father died.' His mother's soft voice penetrated the sluggish fog of his mind. 'You were always so serious. So *controlled*. But somehow you were still able to make us laugh.'

She offered him a sad smile that held a wealth of remembered pain.

'I can see now it was your way of dealing with your pain, and I'm sorry I wasn't there more for you right after it happened.'

Valentino raked an unsteady hand through his hair. 'He always acted so bloody invincible and I...' He swallowed the sudden lump in his throat. 'I stupidly believed him.'

'Oh, darling. I'm so sorry. And I must have only made it worse by relying on you so heavily after his death because I thought you understood.'

Valentino felt something release and peel open deep inside him. Clasping his mother's shoulders, he drew her into his arms. 'I'm not angry at you, Ma.'

'Not any more, hmmm?'

He heard her sniff and tightened his embrace. 'I'm sorry. I've been an ass to you and to Tom. I treated him appallingly when he dutifully drove me to go-cart meets every month, stood in the wings of every damned race.' He stopped, unable to express his remorse at the way he had treated his mother's second husband.

His mother hugged him tight. 'He understood.'

'Then he's a better man than I am.'

'You were only sixteen when we married—a difficult age at the best of times.'

'I think I resented him because he was around when Dad just never had been.'

'Your father took his responsibilities seriously, Valentino. His problem was that he'd grown up in a cold household and didn't know how to express love. He didn't know how to show you that he loved you, but he was torn. That morning...' She stopped, swallowed. 'We'd been talking a lot about him retiring leading up to that awful race, and I think that had he survived he *would* have quit.'

'I overheard you both talking about it that morning.'

His mother closed her eyes briefly. 'Then you must blame me for his death. For putting him off his race.'

Her voice quavered and Tino rushed to reassure her. 'No. Certainly not. Honestly, I blamed Dad for trying to have it all. I think, if anything, I was just upset that you hadn't tried to stop him.'

His mother pulled back and gave him a wistful smile. 'It is what it is. We are each defined by the choices that we make for good and bad. And it wasn't an easy decision for your father to make. He had sponsors breathing down his neck, the team owner, his fans. He did his best, but fate had other ideas.' She paused. 'But life goes on, and I've been lucky enough to find love not once, but twice in my life. I hope you get to experience the same thing at least once. I hope all of my children do.'

Jamming his hands in his pockets, Tino wished he could jam a lid on the emotions swirling through his brain.

Damn Miller. She had been right. He had been angry with his mother all this time. 'I'm sorry. Thank you for telling me.'

He caught a movement in his peripheral vision and saw Tom,

his stepfather, about to head back inside, his expression clearly showing that he didn't want to interrupt.

Valentino beckoned him and Tom approached, putting his arm around his wife, love shining brightly in his eyes. 'I didn't want to interrupt.'

Tino drew in a long, unsteady breath. 'Tom…' He searched for a way to thank this man he had previously disdained for loving his mother and always being there for him and his siblings.

Tom inclined his head in a brief nod. 'We're good.'

Tino felt a parody of a smile twist his mouth. He nodded at Tom, kissed his mother's cheek and left them to admire the view.

The urge to throw down a finger of whisky was intense. So was the need to find Miller.

Tino did neither.

Instead, he took the lift to the ground floor and hailed a cab to the only place he'd ever found real peace.

His car.

The tight security team at the Albert Park raceway were surprised to see him, but no one stopped him from entering.

Not ever having been in the pits this late at night, he was surprised with how eerie it felt. Everything was deadly quiet. The monitors were off, the cars tucked away under protective cloth. The air was still, with only a faint trace of gasoline and rubber.

He threw the protective covering off his car, pulled the steering wheel out and climbed in. His body immediately relaxed into the bucket seat designed specifically to fit his shape. The scent of moulded plastic and polish was instantly soothing.

After re-fixing the steering wheel, he did an automatic pre-race check on the buttons and knobs.

Then he thought of his father and the times he'd watched him do the same thing, remembering the connection they had shared.

He released a long breath, realising that he had always felt superior to his father because *he'd* kept everyone at a safe distance. He'd believed it to be one of his great strengths, but maybe he'd been wrong.

A faint memory flickered at the edges of his mind, and he let his head fall back, stared unseeing at the high metal ceiling. What was his mind trying to tell him...? Oh, yeah—his father had once told him that when love hit you'd better watch out, because you didn't have any say in the matter. You just had to go for it.

Tino's hands tensed around the steering wheel. His father hadn't been weak, as he'd assumed, he'd been strong. He'd dared to have it all. Okay, he'd made mistakes along the way, but did that make him a bad person?

In a moment of true clarity, Tino realised that he was little more than an arrogant, egotistical shmuck. One who didn't dare love because he was afraid to open himself up to the pain he had experienced at losing his father.

For years he'd truly believed he was unable to experience deep emotion, but now he realised that was just a ruse—because Miller had cracked him open and wormed her way into his head and his heart.

Damn.

Tino banged the steering wheel as the truth of his feelings for her stared him in the face. He loved Miller. Loved her as he'd never wanted to love anyone. And ironically he was now faced with his worst nightmare. Forced to face the same decision he'd held his father to account for so many years ago.

For so long he had resented his father for refusing to quit, but he'd had no right to feel that way. No right to stand in judgement of a man who'd been driven to please everyone.

Like Miller.

Tino felt a stillness settle over him.

He could hear tomorrow's crowd already, smell the gasoline in the air, the burn of rubber on asphalt, *feel* the vibration of the car surrounding him, drawing him into a place that was almost spiritual. But despite all that he couldn't *see* himself doing it.

He could only see Miller. Miller in the bar in her black suit.

Miller tapping her toes by the car as she waited for him to pick her up. Miller completely wild for him on the beach, in his bed, staring at him with wide, hurt eyes in the ballroom as the light from the chandeliers lit sparks in her wavy hair.

God, he was more of an idiot than Caruthers. He'd had her, she'd been *his*, and he'd pushed her away. Closed her down as he'd done all week whenever the conversation had veered towards anything too personal.

Levering himself out of his car, he knew he was saying goodbye to a part of his life that had sustained him for so long, but one that he didn't need any more.

He didn't care what the naysayers would say when he pulled out of the race tomorrow. For the first time ever he had too much to lose to go out onto the track. For the first time ever he wanted something else more.

The signs had been there. Or maybe they hadn't been signs, maybe they'd just been coincidences. It didn't matter. When he closed his eyes and thought about his future he wasn't standing on a podium, holding up yet another trophy. He was with Miller.

Miller who had stalked off with tears behind her eyes.

Where *was* she?

He doubted she'd organised the jet to fly back to Sydney at this late hour; she was too considerate to disturb his pilot.

Likely she was still at the hotel. But he'd bet everything he owned she'd arranged for another room by now.

Miller felt terrible. Beyond terrible. Walking away from Valentino's offer to travel with him had felt like the hardest thing she had ever done in her life. Even harder than leaving her father behind in Queensland all those years ago.

She was in love with Valentino and she was never going to see him again, never going to touch him again. There was something fundamentally wrong with that.

Travel with me. Come to Monaco next week.

Had she made a monumental mistake?

Miller looked down, half expecting to find herself standing

on a trapdoor that would open up at any minute and put her out of her misery, but instead all that was there was designer carpet.

She sighed. This morning she had woken in Valentino's arms and felt that life couldn't get any better. TJ had signed Oracle to consult for his company *before* finding out what Valentino's decision about Real Sport was, and the powers-that-be had requested a meeting with her first thing Monday morning. Which could only mean a promotion because, as Ruby had pointed out, no one got fired on a Monday.

But the idea of a promotion didn't mean half as much as it once might have. Not only because her priorities had changed over the course of the week, but because she felt as if all the colour had been leached out of her life. Try as she might to pull herself together, it seemed her heart had taken a firm hold of her head and it was miserable. Aching.

She'd known falling in love would be a mistake, and boy had she ever been right about that. Love was terrible. Painful. *Horrible.*

She had accused Valentino of keeping himself safe from this kind of pain, but of course it was what she had always done as well. Keeping her hair straight, wearing black, hiding herself away at her work in an attempt to control her life. None of it had been real—just like her relationship with Valentino.

Only towards the end it had felt real with him. Had *become* real without her even noticing... She'd fallen in love and he hadn't. Which just went to prove the law of relationships: one person always felt more.

And now, sitting on Valentino's plane as his pilot ran through the preflight check, still wearing her beautiful, frothy dress, she felt like the heroine from a tragic novel.

She sniffed back tears and wondered if she had time to put her casual clothes on. And then she wondered what was taking so long. Surely she'd been sitting on the tarmac for over an hour now?

The whoosh of the outer doors opening brought her head

round, and she was startled to see Valentino's broad shoulders filling the doorway.

Like her, he hadn't taken the time to change, and he looked impossibly virile: his bow tie was hanging loosely around his neck and the top buttons of his dress shirt were reefed open.

Miller swallowed, her heart thumping in her chest. 'What are you doing here?'

Valentino stalked inside the small cabin. 'Looking for you. And I have to say this is the last place I tried.'

'I told Mickey not to tell you.'

'He didn't. My pilot did.'

He looked annoyed.

'I'm sorry if you're upset about me commandeering your plane at this hour. I felt terrible doing it. But all the hotel rooms were booked and Mickey insisted...'

'I don't care about the plane. And stop moving.' Miller stopped when she realised she was stepping backwards. 'Where are you going, anyway?'

'The pilot stowed my bag in the rear cupboard. I was just going to get it.'

'Leave the damn bag.' He dragged a hand through his hair and Miller realised how tired he looked.

She swallowed heavily. 'Why were you looking for me?'

Had she forgotten something? Left something in their room?

'Because I realised after you left that I loved you and I needed to tell you.'

'You...what?'

He came towards her again and Miller's back bumped the cabin wall. Her senses were stunned at his announcement.

Valentino stepped into her personal space and cupped her elbows in his hands. 'You heard right. I love you, Miller. I've spent my whole life convincing myself it was the last thing I wanted, but fortunately you came along and proved me wrong.'

Miller tried to still her galloping heart. 'You told me that racing was all you ever needed.'

'Which shows you that you need to add stupidity to my list of flaws.'

'I might have been a bit harsh earlier.'

'No, you weren't.' He hesitated. 'After my father died I was determined never to love anyone because I convinced myself that I wanted to protect them from the hurt I had experienced. But you were right. I was protecting myself.' He shook his head. 'Until you came into my life, Miller, I truly believed that I didn't have the capacity to love anyone.'

Miller felt her heart swell in her chest. She desperately wanted to believe that he loved her but her old fears wouldn't let go.

He squeezed her hands gently. 'You're thinking something. What is it?'

'I thought you always knew what I was thinking?' Miller smiled weakly at her attempt at humour.

'Usually I do, but right now...I'm too scared to guess.'

Scared? Valentino was *scared*?

His admission was raw, and unbridled hope sparked deep inside her. 'You risk your life every time you race.'

He laughed. 'That's nothing compared to this. Now tell me what you're thinking, baby.'

Miller felt as if her heart had a tractor beam of sunlight shining right at it at the softness of his tone. 'I'm thinking that I may never outgrow my need for certainty, and I don't know if I can watch you throw yourself around a track every other week without making you feel guilty. Watching you qualify today, I thought I was going to throw up.'

'You won't have to do either. I've organised a meeting first thing tomorrow morning to announce my retirement from the circuit. Effective immediately.'

Miller didn't try to hide her shock. 'Why would you do that? You love racing.'

'I love you more.'

His words made her heart leap. 'But what will you do instead?'

'Andy and I have a patent over the new go-cart designs and we have visions of taking Go Wild global. I like your idea of turning it into a venue for corporations to use and I'm also thinking we can use it as a place to give kids interested in competing some personal coaching.'

Miller nodded. 'That's a great idea.'

Valentino blew out a breath as if her opinion really mattered. 'Good. I'm glad you like it. In fact, I was hoping to convince you to consult for us. Andy and I know a lot about cars, but we know jack about running a business.'

'You want me to work for you?' Miller knew she was smiling like a loon.

'Only if you want to—God, Miller, you're beautiful.' Valentino dropped her hands and hauled her against him, kissing her so passionately she couldn't think straight.

He drew back, shuddering. 'Where was I? Oh, yeah. Marry me.'

'Marry you?'

'I'm sorry I don't have a ring yet. Honestly, I've been fighting my feelings so hard for so long I'm embarrassingly underprepared, but I promise to make it up to you.'

Remembering how everything had gone so wrong between them just hours earlier, Miller felt some of her anxiety return.

As if sensing her tumultuous emotions, Valentino tugged her in against him again. 'If you don't like the idea that's fine. I know you have your own dreams to follow and I'll support you in whatever they are.' He smiled. 'Just so long as we find a little bit of time to have a house full of kids.'

'A house full?'

'You said you didn't like being an only child.'

'I hated it.' Miller's head was reeling.

'Then we should probably try for more than one, because chances are they'll hate it too.'

Once again happiness threatened to engulf her, but a tiny niggle of doubt still prevailed. 'Wait. You're steamrollering me again.'

'But I am wearing a suit this time. Does that count?'

Miller felt both fearful and excited in the face of his unwavering resolve. 'It does help that you look insanely handsome in one, yes.'

Valentino clasped her face in his hands. 'Okay, you're still worried. Talk to me.'

Miller wet her dry lips and took a deep breath. He'd put his heart on the line for her, was giving up his racing career to be with her. The least she could do was confide her greatest fear.

'Valentino, you can't possibly feel the same way about me as I do about you, and that will eventually ruin everything between us.'

She tried to glance away, feeling utterly miserable now, but he held her fast.

'How *do* you feel about me, Miller?'

'I love you, of course. But—'

She didn't get any further as his mouth captured hers in a blistering kiss so full of sensual passion and promise that tears stung the backs of her eyes.

'Stop.' She pushed at him weakly, her body trembling against his. 'You're too good at that, and it doesn't change the fundamental law of relationships.'

'Which one's that?' he asked, nuzzling the side of her neck.

Miller tried to put some distance between them, but his hold was implacable. 'The one that says one person will always love more than the other.'

Her voice was so anguished Valentino stopped kissing her and stared into her eyes. 'I've never heard of that law, but you'll never love me as much as I love you. I guarantee it.'

'No.' Miller shook her head. 'Your feelings can't possibly be as strong as mine are for you.'

Valentino smiled, pressed her against the cabin wall. 'Want to argue about it for the rest of our lives?'

Miller burst out laughing, radiant happiness slowly soaking into every corner of her heart. 'You're serious!'

Valentino stayed her nervous hands in one of his. 'I've never been more serious about anything. I once told you I'd never met a woman who excited me as much as racing—but, Miller, you do. I feel exhilarated just thinking about seeing you. And when I do...' He shook his head, the depth of his emotions shining brightly in his eyes.

Miller gazed back at the only man who had ever made her heart sing. 'I love you *so* much. I didn't know it was even possible to feel like this about another person.'

'Ditto, Sunshine. Now, put me out of my misery and tell me you'll marry me.'

Completely overwhelmed by emotions no longer held at bay Miller grinned stupidly. 'I'll marry you—but with one condition.'

Valentino groaned. 'I knew you wouldn't make it easy. What's the condition?'

Miller linked her hands behind his neck, deciding to have some fun with him. 'We do it at my pace, *not* yours.'

Valentino threw back his head and laughed. 'I told Sam that was my lucky shirt. Now it will be forever known as my *life-changing* shirt.'

Wriggling closer, Miller nuzzled his neck, the last of her doubts fading into nothing. 'I love you.'

Valentino's touch became purposeful, masterful. 'And I you.'

Miller smiled. How had she ever thought love was horrible? Love was w*onderful.*

* * * * *

Mills & Boon® Hardback

February 2013

ROMANCE

Sold to the Enemy	Sarah Morgan
Uncovering the Silveri Secret	Melanie Milburne
Bartering Her Innocence	Trish Morey
Dealing Her Final Card	Jennie Lucas
In the Heat of the Spotlight	Kate Hewitt
No More Sweet Surrender	Caitlin Crews
Pride After Her Fall	Lucy Ellis
Living the Charade	Michelle Conder
The Downfall of a Good Girl	Kimberly Lang
The One That Got Away	Kelly Hunter
Her Rocky Mountain Protector	Patricia Thayer
The Billionaire's Baby SOS	Susan Meier
Baby out of the Blue	Rebecca Winters
Ballroom to Bride and Groom	Kate Hardy
How To Get Over Your Ex	Nikki Logan
Must Like Kids	Jackie Braun
The Brooding Doc's Redemption	Kate Hardy
The Son that Changed his Life	Jennifer Taylor

MEDICAL

An Inescapable Temptation	Scarlet Wilson
Revealing The Real Dr Robinson	Dianne Drake
The Rebel and Miss Jones	Annie Claydon
Swallowbrook's Wedding of the Year	Abigail Gordon

0113 GEN STD HB

Mills & Boon® Large Print
February 2013

ROMANCE

Banished to the Harem	Carol Marinelli
Not Just the Greek's Wife	Lucy Monroe
A Delicious Deception	Elizabeth Power
Painted the Other Woman	Julia James
Taming the Brooding Cattleman	Marion Lennox
The Rancher's Unexpected Family	Myrna Mackenzie
Nanny for the Millionaire's Twins	Susan Meier
Truth-Or-Date.com	Nina Harrington
A Game of Vows	Maisey Yates
A Devil in Disguise	Caitlin Crews
Revelations of the Night Before	Lynn Raye Harris

HISTORICAL

Two Wrongs Make a Marriage	Christine Merrill
How to Ruin a Reputation	Bronwyn Scott
When Marrying a Duke...	Helen Dickson
No Occupation for a Lady	Gail Whitiker
Tarnished Rose of the Court	Amanda McCabe

MEDICAL

Sydney Harbour Hospital: Ava's Re-Awakening	Carol Marinelli
How To Mend A Broken Heart	Amy Andrews
Falling for Dr Fearless	Lucy Clark
The Nurse He Shouldn't Notice	Susan Carlisle
Every Boy's Dream Dad	Sue MacKay
Return of the Rebel Surgeon	Connie Cox

ROMANCE

MEDICAL

Mills & Boon® Large Print
March 2013

ROMANCE

A Night of No Return	Sarah Morgan
A Tempestuous Temptation	Cathy Williams
Back in the Headlines	Sharon Kendrick
A Taste of the Untamed	Susan Stephens
The Count's Christmas Baby	Rebecca Winters
His Larkville Cinderella	Melissa McClone
The Nanny Who Saved Christmas	Michelle Douglas
Snowed in at the Ranch	Cara Colter
Exquisite Revenge	Abby Green
Beneath the Veil of Paradise	Kate Hewitt
Surrendering All But Her Heart	Melanie Milburne

HISTORICAL

How to Sin Successfully	Bronwyn Scott
Hattie Wilkinson Meets Her Match	Michelle Styles
The Captain's Kidnapped Beauty	Mary Nichols
The Admiral's Penniless Bride	Carla Kelly
Return of the Border Warrior	Blythe Gifford

MEDICAL

Her Motherhood Wish	Anne Fraser
A Bond Between Strangers	Scarlet Wilson
Once a Playboy...	Kate Hardy
Challenging the Nurse's Rules	Janice Lynn
The Sheikh and the Surrogate Mum	Meredith Webber
Tamed by her Brooding Boss	Joanna Neil